j398.2
R

ROSS, Eulalie Steinmetz
THE BURIED TREASURE, AND OTHER PICTURE
TALES. Illustrated by Josef Cellini.
Philadelphia, Lippincott ₍1958₎ 187p.
illus. 3.00
1. FABLES 2. FOLKLORE 3. TALES

Related
Books In
Catalog
Under

* Ages 8-10

Ja 63   Title.

The Buried Treasure
AND OTHER PICTURE TALES

The Buried Treasure
and Other Picture Tales

SELECTED BY
Eulalie Steinmetz Ross

ILLUSTRATED BY
Josef Cellini

PHILADELPHIA   J. B. Lippincott Company   NEW YORK

Illustrations and Foreword Copyright © 1958
by J. B. Lippincott Company

"The Frog" and "The Flea" were previously published in PIC-
TURE TALES FROM SPAIN, by Ruth Sawyer, copyright 1936
by J. B. Lippincott Company. "The People of Mols" and "The
Buried Treasure" were previously published in PICTURE
TALES FROM SCANDINAVIA, by Ruth Bryan Owen, copy-
right 1939 by J. B. Lippincott Company. "The Talkative King"
and "The Banyan Deer" were previously published in PICTURE
TALES FROM INDIA, by Berta Metzger, copyright 1942 by
J. B. Lippincott Company. "Señor Coyote Settles a Quarrel" and
"The War Between the Lion and the Cricket" were previously
published in PICTURE TALES FROM MEXICO, by Dan
Storm, copyright 1941 by J. B. Lippincott Company. "The Little
Bucket" and "The Eagle and the Owl" were previously pub-
lished in PICTURE TALES FROM THE ITALIAN, by Flor-
ence Botsford, copyright 1929 by F. H. Botsford, 1957 by Rosa-
mond Marshall. "Little Cricket" was previously published in
PICTURE TALES FROM THE FRENCH, by Simone Chamoud,
copyright 1933 by Simone Chamoud. "Jan and Jaantje" and
"The Magic Cap" were previously published in PICTURE
TALES FROM HOLLAND, by Johan Hart, copyright 1935 by
J. B. Lippincott Company. "How the Camel Got His Proud
Look" and "The Golden Boat" were previously published in
PICTURE TALES FROM THE CHINESE, by Berta Metzger,
copyright 1934 by J. B. Lippincott Company. "The Peach Boy,"
"The Good-Luck Teakettle" and "Urashima" were previously
published in PICTURE TALES FROM THE JAPANESE, by
Chiyono Sugimoto, copyright 1928, 1956 by Chiyono Sugimoto.

Printed in the United States of America
Second Impression
Library of Congress Catalog Card Number 58-7532

To

A. G. R.

FOREWORD

For many years as a children's librarian in Cincinnati and New York City I watched boys and girls carry lovingly from public libraries the distinctive rectangular little books of the *Picture Tales* series: *Picture Tales from the Russian, Picture Tales from Spain, Japanese Picture Tales, Picture Tales from Mexico* and so on—around the world with picture tales. As a storyteller in both cities I told and heard told many of the stories from the same books. To be asked, then, to make a selection from the books, now out-of-print, so that children and storytellers might still enjoy them was a genuine pleasure.

As I re-read the stories, the reading was accompanied by the echo of storytellers' voices and children's laughter; by the memory of eyes deep with wonder, mouths stretched with grins. How the little children delighted in the cheeky impudence of Mr. Bun with his most remarkable genealogy! How an inspired storyteller, with a truly feline sound, made Mr. Samson Cat seem every bit as ferocious and large as the hare thought him to be! How a group of children relaxed with a guest storyteller, completely at ease, because of their shared laughter over the ridiculous antics of the people of Mols! How an Irish librarian rollicked her way through "The Flea" with complete confidence for, after all, is not riddling an amusement the world over?

All of the stories in this collection have similar memories behind them. In a sense, it was the children and the storytellers of The Cincinnati Public Library and The New York Public Library who made the selection of stories for this book: the editor just remembered their listening and their telling.

The original authors of the individual titles in the *Picture Tales* series were all peculiarly fitted for their tasks by birth, by travel, or by residence in the various countries represented in the *Tales*. They heard the stories told; they knew the people who told them; their ears were attuned to the rhythm and lilt of the storyteller's voice; their source material was vital and alive: it was *folk*. How else to gather *folk* tales?

Because of their source, in part, folk tales have a certain universality of theme, a fact most surely apparent to the original collectors of the *Tales*. Children became aware of this by reading the stories so gathered for them from France, Italy, Scandinavia, India, Holland, China—from countries all over the world. For in the stories of the *Picture Tales* there was One World where the simplest truths were the eternal ones, where man laughed and wept and wondered with man.

It is my earnest hope that boys and girls will be able to sense that same oneness in this selection of stories from the *Tales*, either by reading the book themselves or by having the stories brought to life for them through the art of storytelling.

Eulalie Steinmetz Ross

July 18, 1957

CONTENTS

Russia

Spain

Scandinavia

India

Mexico

Italy

France

Holland

China

Japan

The Buried Treasure

AND OTHER PICTURE TALES

The Bun

FROM

PICTURE TALES FROM THE RUSSIAN

By Valery Carrick

Once upon a time there was an old man, and one day he wanted something nice to eat, so he said to his wife, "My dear, please make me a bun."

But she answered, "What am I to make it of? We have no flour."

"What nonsense," he said, "of course we have! You've only got to scrape the sides of the bin and sweep its floor and you'll get plenty!"

So his wife took a feather brush, and scraped the sides and swept the floor of the bin, and got a little flour together. Then she kneaded the dough with cream, rolled out the bun, spread it over with butter and put it in the oven.

And the bun turned out simply splendid! She took it out of the oven and put it on the window sill to get cold.

And there the bun lay and lay, and he began to feel lonely, so he just took and rolled off!

From the window sill he rolled down onto the bench, from the bench onto the floor, and over the floor to the door.

Then he rolled right over the threshold into the lobby, out of the lobby onto the front doorsteps and down the steps right out of doors, and rolled straight along the road into the field.

Suddenly he met a hare, and the hare said to him, "Mr. Bun, Mr. Bun I shall eat you up!"

"No you shan't, Mr. Hare, for I'll sing you a song." And he started singing: "I'm Mr. Bun, I'm Mr. Bun, I was scraped from the sides and swept from the floor of the bin, I was kneaded with cream and fried in butter, and was put to cool on the window sill, but I got away from gaffer and I got away from grannie, and I shan't find it hard to get away from you!" And when he had finished his song he went rolling farther, and was out of sight before Mr. Hare had time to look.

And he went on rolling, when suddenly he met a wolf, and the wolf said to him, "Mr. Bun, Mr. Bun, I shall eat you up!"

"No you shan't, Mr. Wolf, for I'll sing you a song." And he started singing: "I'm Mr. Bun, I'm Mr. Bun, I was scraped from the sides and swept from the floor of the bin, I was kneaded with cream and fried in butter, and was put to cool on the window sill, but I got away from gaffer and I got away from grannie, and I got away from Mr. Hare, and I think I'll find it easy enough to get away from you!"

And he went on rolling farther, when suddenly he met a bear. And the bear said to him, "Mr. Bun, Mr. Bun, I shall eat you up!"

"Indeed you shall not, you old crooked-paws, you couldn't if you tried." And he started singing: "For I'm Mr. Bun, I'm Mr. Bun, I was scraped from the sides, and swept from the floor of the bin, I was kneaded with cream and fried in butter, and was put to cool on the window sill, but I got away from gaffer and I got away from grannie, I got away from Mr. Hare, and got away from Mr. Wolf—Good-bye, Bruin!"

And he went on rolling farther, when suddenly he met a fox, and the fox said to him, "How do you do, Mr. Bun, how pretty you are and how well-baked you are!"

And Mr. Bun, was pleased at being praised, and he started singing: "I'm Mr. Bun, I'm Mr. Bun, I was scraped from the sides and swept from the floor of the bin, I was kneaded with cream and fried in butter, and was put to cool on the window sill, but I got away from gaffer and I got away from grannie, I got away from Mr. Hare, and got away from Mr. Wolf, I got away from Bruin and I'll get away from you!"

"*That's* a fine song," said the fox, "please sing it to me again, but come and sit on my nose, I've got so deaf lately."

So Mr. Bun jumped up on Mr. Fox's nose and sang his song again.

And the fox said, "Thank you, Mr. Bun, but please sing it just once again. And come and sit on my tongue, then I shall hear still better." And Mr.

Fox put out his tongue and Mr. Bun jumped on to it, and Mr. Fox just closed his mouth and ate Mr. Bun up.

Mr. Samson Cat

FROM

PICTURE TALES FROM THE RUSSIAN

By Valery Carrick

Once upon a time a cat came running out
of a certain village, and a fox came running out of
a certain forest, and they met.

"How do you do?" said the fox.

"How do you do?" said the cat.

"What's your name?" said the fox.

"Mr. Samson Cat, and what's yours?"

"They call me Widow Fox."

"Let's live together," said the cat.

"Very well," said the fox. And so they settled down in Widow Fox's cottage.

One day Mr. Cat went out for a walk to gather berries in the forest, when a hare came running along. He never noticed the cat and jumped right onto the top of him.

Mr. Cat said, "F-r-r-r!" and the hare took fright and set off running so fast, that you could just see his heels twinkle, and he was gone!

Then the hare met a wolf, and said to him, "As I was running past Widow Fox's cottage, an unheard-of beast jumped right onto the top of me; he was so big and so dreadful! He was just going to swallow me up alive, only my legs saved me!"

"I must go and have a look," said the wolf.

"Don't, he will eat you up!" said the hare. Nevertheless the wolf went off to Widow Fox's cottage. And just then Widow Fox and Mr. Samson Cat had dragged a dead sheep into their courtyard, and were hard at it behind the fence, gobbling him up.

When Widow Fox had had enough, she came out at the gate, and there Mr. Wolf came up to her. He could hear how Mr. Cat was going on behind the fence, and said to Widow Fox, "Who is that there in your courtyard, Widow Fox?"

"That's the mighty Mr. Samson Cat. He killed a sheep in a fight and now he's eating it. You'd better go away quickly, or else the same thing will happen to you."

Meantime Mr. Cat was working hard at the sheep and crying, "Mee-*ow*, Mee-*ow!*"

And Mr. Wolf thought he was saying, "Not *enough,* not *enough,*" and he thought; "Good gracious, he hasn't had enough after eating a whole sheep!" and he grew frightened and ran away. And as he was running he saw a pig rubbing his side against a tree. And he said to him, "Have you heard the news? We shan't be able to make a living in *this* forest any more; Widow Fox has got a dreadful animal living with her, the mighty Mr. Samson Cat. He eats four sheep a day, and then says he hasn't had enough."

And Mr. Pig flapped his ears and winked his eye and said, "I should like to have a look at this beast!"

"What are you thinking of?" said Mr. Wolf, "you'd better not go near the place!"

And while they were standing and talking, a bear came up, and Mr. Pig said to him, "Uncle Bruin, have you heard the news? Widow Fox has a beast living with her called the mighty Mr. Samson Cat. He eats ten oxen a day, and then says he hasn't had enough!"

"What a terrible thing," said Bruin, "I *should* like to see that beast!"

So they discussed this way and that, and sent Mr. Pig to Widow Fox to ask if they might just with one eye have a peep at Mr. Samson Cat. And Mr. Pig came to Widow Fox and said, "How do you do? how do you do, Widow Fox? We have heard tell of your Mr. Samson and we should so like to have a look at him. Do please tell us how this could be arranged without the danger of his eating us up!"

And Widow Fox thought for a bit and then said, "This is how you must arrange it: bake a *lot* of pies and get a *lot* of honey, and invite us to come and see you. *Perhaps* he won't do you any harm then."

And Mr. Pig was delighted and ran back to his friends and told Mr. Wolf and Mr. Bruin, "Widow Fox says: 'Bake a *lot* of pies and get a *lot* of honey, and we will come and see you, and *perhaps* the mighty Mr. Samson Cat won't eat you all up.' " And so Bruin began to get the honey, Mr. Wolf began to bake the pies, and Mr. Pig began to tidy up, and get ready to receive the expected guests.

And they baked a *lot* of pies, and got a *lot* of honey, and Bruin said, "I shall get up into a tree; from there I shall see better when the guests begin to arrive." And so he climbed up.

And Mr. Wolf said, "For a whole day I've been working at those pies. I shall go and rest for a bit under this log." And he crawled under the log and lay down there.

And Mr. Pig said, "I have got hot all over, making everything tidy. I shall go and get into the shade for a bit." And he went and hid in the brushwood.

Meanwhile Widow Fox and the mighty Mr. Samson Cat came along, and their hosts were not there! Bruin was up an oak, Mr. Wolf under a log, and Mr. Pig in the brushwood. So there was nothing to be done but start eating without their hosts, and Widow Fox went for the honey, while Mr. Cat got to work on the stuffed pies.

Suddenly Mr. Cat heard something rustling in the grass, and this was Mr. Pig's tail, rustling from fright. Mr. Cat thought: "I expect that's a mouse," and dashed off and caught Mr. Pig by the tail.

Mr. Pig squealed and ran off as hard as he could,

and ran his snout straight into the stump of a tree.

Mr. Cat was really just as much frightened himself, and jumped onto the tree. At this Bruin's paws grew weak from fright, and he fell plump down from the tree right onto the top of the log under which Mr. Wolf was lying.

And Mr. Wolf thought: "My end has come," and he jumped out from under the log and started off running as hard as he could go. And it was not till evening that Mr. Wolf, Mr. Pig and Bruin met again and told each other the⸱ ⸱ ⸱ riences.

Mr. Pig said, "Well I   way he caught hold of my tail and dasi⸱ ⸱ ⸱   ⸱ad against the stump!"

And Bruin said, "The stump was nothing! He tore out the whole oak tree by the roots and began to shake it. How could I possibly hold on? I was lucky not to fall into his jaws."

And Mr. Wolf said, "And the way he put me one on with that oak tree! Well, that *is* a beast, if you like!"

And they all began to shake their heads and said, "Well, that *is* a beast, if you like! There's no mistake about Mr. Samson Cat!"

Snowflake

FROM

PICTURE TALES FROM THE RUSSIAN

By Valery Carrick

Once upon a time in a certain village there lived an old man and his wife. They wanted to have a little daughter, but alas! they hadn't got one.

One day the old man saw how the children were making a snowman out of snow, and he said to his wife, "Look here, my dear, let's go and make a little girl out of snow; we'll call her Snowflake and she'll be like a little daughter to us." And they went off and began to make her. And they made a little girl out of the snow, and she was simply lovely. And she began to laugh and move her arms and legs about, and came to life. And the old man and his wife took her to their hut and gave her plenty to eat and drink; and she grew up quite a big girl.

Snowflake was quite a nice little girl, only she couldn't stand the heat. Whenever the old woman lit the oven and put her pots with porridge and soup into it, and let the heat out into the room, Snowflake took it into her head to go out into the passage, where she felt better.

Then came the spring, the sun began to grow hot, and all the snow melted. But Snowflake wasn't at all pleased at this.

Her little friends would all go playing in the sunshine, running barefoot in the puddles, and plashing about in the water, but Snowflake would choose a shady corner in the house, where she sat playing with her dolls while it was hot out of doors.

Then the flowers all blossomed in the fields, and the berries began to grow ripe. Snowflake's little friends wanted her to go walking with them in the forest under the shady trees, and play all sorts of games. Snowflake didn't want to go, but they kept

on so that at last she said she would.

And they all ran and played about in the forest till they were tired. Then they lit a fire, and began to jump over it for fun. And when Snowflake's turn came to jump, she jumped—and lo and behold! she melted in the fire and went up like a little white cloud into the air.

The Little House

FROM

PICTURE TALES FROM THE RUSSIAN

By Valery Carrick

Once upon a time a jar rolled off a peasant's cart, and was left lying in the middle of a field. And a little mouse came running along and saw the jar lying there, and thought what a nice house it would make, and began to wonder who lived there.

And the little mouse said, "Little house, little house, who lives in the little house?"

And nobody answered. Then the little mouse

looked in, and found no one there!   "Well then," he said, "I shall live here myself." So he settled himself in the jar.

Then a frog came hopping along, and said, "Little house, little house, who lives in the little house?"

"I, Mr. Mouse, I live in the little house, and what sort of animal are you?"

"I am Mr. Frog."

"Come inside, then, and let's live together."

"Very well, let's." So the frog crept into the jar, and they began to live together.

Then a hare came running over the field. "Little house, little house," said he, "who lives in the little house?"

"Mr. Frog and Mr. Mouse, and who are you?"

"I am Mr. Hare who runs over the hills. May I come in, too?"

"Yes, you may; come and live here, there's plenty of room."

Then a fox came running past, and said, "Little house, little house, who lives in the little house?"

"Mr. Hare, Mr. Frog, and Mr. Mouse. And what is *your* name?"

"They call me Mr. Fox."

"Very well, then, come and live with us."

"Right you are!" So the fox got into the jar too, and all four began to live together.

And they went on living there, when suddenly a bear came along out of the forest, and said, "Little house, little house, who lives in the little house."

"Mr. Fox, Mr. Hare, Mr. Frog, and Mr. Mouse; and who are you?"

"I am Mr. Bear-Squash-you-all-flat!"

And the bear sat down on the jar and squashed it flat.

The Frog

FROM

PICTURE TALES FROM SPAIN

By Ruth Sawyer

Once there lived a peasant whom his neighbors called Perico. He had a small but fertile *finca*. He loved the earth; he raised the good carrots, the white onions, the excellent cabbages, and the green spinaches for those who liked them.

He had a wife and nine *pequeños;* and when there were vegetables left from the family table he took them to market and sold them for silver which bought many things that were needed.

One morning Perico woke early. "Today I am going to market," he told his wife.

"*Si Dios quiere*—if God wills," corrected his wife.

"There are a hundred carrots, a thousand onions, baskets of spinach. We need silver. I am going whether God wills or not."

All the time that he was putting the harness with brass bells and red tassels on Chorlito, the small gray donkey, and fastening him to the small two-wheeled cart, his wife stood at his side talking to him. "Husband, you must say it. Please. Say it even if you say it to no one but Chorlito."

"I will not say it. *Arre, burrito,*" he said to the donkey. He touched his ear with the end of his whip and they were off. His wife turned sorrowfully into the doorway. What was the use of shouting after him—"Go with God!" God would never follow the road with such a sinner.

Down the road that winds along the muddy river to Seville went Perico, the gray donkey, the little cart piled high with its baskets of vegetables. They fell in with another peasant, riding his donkey to be shod. "Where are you going?" he asked.

"I go to market."

"Ay, truly, you go to market—*si Dios quiere.*"

"I go whether God wills or not," and Perico lashed Chorlito with the long whip.

They came up with a water-carrier who gave them good day. "Where are you going?"

"I go to market."

"*Si Dios quiere*—yes?"

"I go whether God wills or not," shouted Perico.

They met the baker taking his hard, round loaves into the country to sell. They met the good *cura* going to baptize a new baby. They met a drove of gypsies on a pilgrimage. To each and all of them he shouted the same answer until he was hoarse, growing more hot and angry with each shouting. "I tell you—the world—for the hundredth time I go to market, to sell my vegetables, whether God wills or not!"

At the start of the bridge that crosses over the river from Triana to Seville he turned Chorlito up the incline and there he was stopped by a traveler with a long cape, well cloaking him, a wide hat of black beaver, shoes thick with the dust of the road, and a staff in his hand.

"Friend, where are you going?" he asked.

Perico looked at him with blazing eyes. "I go to market."

"*Si Dios quiere,* friend."

"Call me not friend; and I go whether God wills or not."

The traveler shot out an arm to stay him. "To-day you speak as stupidly and stubbornly as a frog. Be a frog."

Before Perico could say—"*Basta!*" he found himself on the bank of the river, under the bridge; he was small, wet, green above, yellow underneath—a silly frog. Gone was Chorlito, beloved of donkeys, gone was the two-wheeled cart it had taken him a twelvemonth to build, gone were the good carrots, the white onions, the excellent cabbages, the green spinaches, for those who liked them. He was a frog, accursed. He croaked aloud his misery: "*Ay de mi—ay de mí!*"

A heron flew up the river and screamed at him: "*Si Dios quiere, si Dios quiere, si Dios quiere.*"

Sailors on a ship docked nearby, pulled on the ropes of the rigging and sang together: "Ahoy—to the sea—*si Dios quiere—quiere—quiere.*"

The big bells on the *Giralda* rang out the hour: "Nine o'clock—*si Dios quiere.*"

The frog croaked his misery aloud again. "All of God's world is saying it but me;" and he began to think of the wife and nine *pequeños* at home. "I must get back to them," he thought.

He began jumping up the bank, along the river, northwards. The going was slow—slow. A shadow fell on him, cutting off the sun. He looked far upwards. There stood the traveler, the cape on his shoulders, the hat on his head, the dust on his shoes, the staff in his hand.

"Señor Frog, where are you going?" he asked.

"Back to the wife and the nine *pequeños.*"

"*Si Dios quiere,* yes?"

"Whether God wills or not, I go."

"Go if you must. You will find it a long journey for a frog."

And there he was, back at the bridge again, no distance home at all. He began his jumping along the river. The stones bruised his feet; the sun scorched his back. Noon had passed. He was getting nowhere. A shadow fell again upon him. Looking up he saw the traveler.

"And now, friend, where are you going?"

"Back to the nine *pequeños.*"

"*Si Dios quiere?*"

"If God wills, yes."

"But, I thought you were going to market?"

"To market, yes, if God wills."

"Good. And go with God."

Perico rubbed his eyes. Where was he! Was he going home? Was he going to market? Had he a gray donkey, Chorlito by name? Had he vegetables to sell? Was it morning—was it night?

He sighed enormously and with a great content. He was no longer a frog. He was a man again, with a man's good legs under him. He was on the bridge, not under it. A loud *he-haw* shook the air at his elbow. God be praised—there was Chorlito, the two-wheeled cart, and the vegetables. He was Perico, the peasant, with a wife and nine *pequeños* waiting for him at home. *Basta!* He would buy them for a great surprise some *turrón,* the good candy with its honey and almonds. But about the frog—he would keep that to himself.

The Flea

FROM

PICTURE TALES FROM SPAIN

BY RUTH SAWYER

Once there was and was not a King of Spain. He loved to laugh; he loved a good joke as well as any common fellow. Best of all he loved a riddle.

One day he was being dressed by his chamberlain. As the royal doublet was being slipped over the royal head, a flea jumped from the safe hiding place of the stiff lace ruff. He landed directly upon the King.

Quicker than half a wink the King clapped his hand over the flea and began to laugh. *"Por Dios, a flea!* Who ever heard of a King of Spain having a flea? It is monstrous—it is delicious! We must not treat her lightly, this flea. You perceive, my Lord Chamberlain, that having jumped on the royal person, she has now become a royal flea. Consider what we shall do with her."

But the chamberlain was a man of little wit. He could clothe the King's body but he could not add one ribbon or one button to the King's imagination. "I have it!" said the King at last, exploding again into laughter. "We will pasture out this flea—in a great cage—large enough for a goat—an ox—an elephant. She shall be fed enormously. When she is of a proper size I will have her killed and her skin made into a tambourine. The Infanta, my daughter, shall dance to it. We will make a fine riddle out of it. Whichever suitor that comes courting her who can answer the riddle shall marry with her. *There* is a royal joke worthy of a King! Eh, my Lord Chamberlain? And we will call the flea Felipa."

In his secret heart the chamberlain thought the King quite mad; but all he answered was, "Very -

good, Your Majesty," and went out to see that proper pasturage was provided for Felipa.

At the end of a fortnight the flea was as large as a rat. At the end of a month she was as large as a cat who might have eaten that rat. At the end of a second month she was the size of a dog who might have chased that cat. At the end of three months she was the size of a calf.

The King ordered Felipa killed. The skin was stretched, dried, beaten until it was as soft, as fine, as silk. Then it was made into a tambourine, with brass clappers and ribbons—the finest tambourine in all of Spain.

The Infanta, whose name was Isabel, but who was called Belita for convenience, learned to dance with Felipa very prettily; and the King himself composed a rhyme to go with the riddle. Whenever a suitor came courting, the Infanta would dance and when she had finished, the King would recite:

> "Belita—Felipa—they dance well together—
> Belita—Felipa; now answer me whether
> You know this Felipa—this *animalita*.
> If you answer right, then you marry Belita."

Princes and dukes came from Spain and Portugal,

France and Italy. They were not dull-witted like the chamberlain and they saw through the joke. The King was riddling about the tambourine. It was made from parchment and they knew perfectly well where parchment came from. So a prince would answer, "A goat, Your Majesty." And a duke would answer, "A sheep, Your Majesty"—each sure he was right. And the Infanta would run away laughing and the King would roar with delight and shout, "Wrong again!"

But after a while the King got tired of this sheep and goat business. He wanted the riddle guessed; he wanted the Infanta married. So he sent forth a command that the next suitor who failed to guess the riddle would be hung—and short work made of it, too.

That put a stop to the princes and dukes. But far up in the Castilian highlands a shepherd heard about it. He was young, but not very clever. He thought—it would be a fine thing for a shepherd to marry an Infanta, so he said to his younger brother, "Manuelito—you shall mind the sheep and goats; I will go to the King's palace."

But his mother said, "Son, you are a *tonto*. How should you guess a riddle when you cannot read or write, and those who can, have failed? Stay at home and save yourself a hanging."

Having once made up his mind, nothing would stop him—not even fear. So his mother baked him a *tortilla* to carry with him, gave him her blessing and let him go.

He hadn't gone far when he was stopped by a little black ant. "Señor Pastor," she cried, "give me a ride to the King's court in your pocket."

"La Hormiguita, you cannot ride in my pocket. There is a *tortilla* there which I shall have for my breakfast. Your feet are dirty from walking, and you will tramp all over it."

"See, I will dust off my feet on the grass here and promise not to step once on the *tortilla*."

So the shepherd put the ant into his shepherd pouch and tramped on. Soon he encountered a black beetle who said, "Señor Pastor—give me a ride to the King's court in your pocket."

"El Escarabajo, you cannot ride in my pouch. There is a *tortilla* there which I shall presently have for my breakfast—and who wants a black beetle tramping all over his breakfast!"

"I will fasten my claws into the side of your pouch and not go near the *tortilla*."

So the shepherd took up the beetle and carried him along. He hadn't gone far when he came up with a little gray mouse who cried, "Señor Pastor, give me a ride to the King's court in your pouch."

But the shepherd shook his head. "Ratonperez, you are too clumsy and I don't like the flavor of your breath. It will spoil my *tortilla* that I intend to have for my breakfast."

"Why not eat the *tortilla* now, and then the breakfast will be over and done with," and Ratonperez said it so gently, so coaxingly, that the shepherd thought it was a splendid idea. He sat down and ate it. He gave a little crumb to La Hormiguita, a crumb to El Escarabajo and a big crumb to Ratonperez. Then he went on his road to the King's court carrying the three creatures with him in his pouch.

When he reached the King's palace he was frightened, frightened. He sat himself down under a cork tree to wait for his courage to grow.

"What are you waiting for?" called the ant, the beetle and Ratonperez all together.

"I go to answer a riddle. If I fail I shall be hanged. That isn't so pleasant. So I wait where I can enjoy being alive for a little moment longer."

"What is the riddle?"

"I have heard that it has to do with something called Felipa that dances, whoever she may be."

"Go on and we will help you. Hurry, hurry, it is hot in your pouch."

So the shepherd climbed the palace steps, asked for the King and said that he had come to answer the riddle.

The guard passed him on to the footman, saying, *"Pobrecito!"*

The footman passed him on to the lackey, saying, *"Pobrecito!"*

The lackey passed him on to the court chamberlain, saying, *"Pobrecito!"* And it was his business to present him to the King.

The King shook his head when he saw the shepherd-staff in his hand and the shepherd-pouch hanging from his belt, and he said, "A shepherd's life is better than no life at all. Better go back to your flocks."

But the shepherd was as rich in stubbornness as he was poor in learning. He insisted he must answer the riddle. So the Infanta came and danced with the tambourine and the King laughed and said his rhyme:

"Belita—Felipa—they dance well together—
Belita—Felipa; now answer me whether
You know this Felipa—this *animalita*.
If you answer right, then you marry Belita."

The shepherd strode over and took the tambourine from the hand of the Infanta. He felt the skin carefully, carefully. To himself he said, "I know sheep and I know goats; and it isn't either."

"Can't you guess?" whispered the black beetle from his pouch.

"No," said the shepherd.

"Let me out," said the little ant; "perhaps I can tell you what it is." So the shepherd unfastened the pouch and La Hormiguita crawled out, unseen by the court. She crawled all over the tambourine and came back whispering, "You can't fool me. I'd know a flea anywhere, any size."

"Don't take all day," shouted the King. "Who is Felipa?"

"She's a flea," said the shepherd.

Then the court was in a flutter.

"I don't want to marry a shepherd," said the Infanta.

"You shan't," said the King.

"I'm the one to say 'shan't,' " said the shepherd.

"I will grant you any other favor," said the Infanta.

"I will grant you another," said the King.

"It was a long journey here, walking," said the shepherd. "I would like a cart to ride home in."

"And two oxen to draw it," whispered the black beetle.

"And two oxen to draw it," repeated the shepherd.

"You shall have them," said the King.

"And what shall I give you?" asked the Infanta.

"Tell her you want your pouch filled with gold," whispered Ratonperez.

"That's little enough," said the Infanta.

But while the royal groom was fetching the cart and oxen, and the lord of the exchequer was fetching a bag of gold, Ratonperez was gnawing a hole in the pouch. When they came to pour in the gold, it fell through as fast as water, so that all around the feet of the shepherd it rose like a shining yellow stream.

"That's a lot of gold," said the King at last.

"It's enough," said the shepherd. He took his cart, filled it with the gold, drove back to the highlands of Castile. He married a shepherd's daugh-

ter, who never had to do anything but sit in a
rocking chair and fan herself all day. And that's
a contented life, you might say—for anyone who
likes it.

The People of Mols

FROM

PICTURE TALES FROM SCANDINAVIA

BY RUTH BRYAN OWEN

Many tales were told about the people of Mols, and the funny things they used to do and say.
One day some of them made a trip to the big seaport town, where they stood all day watching the fishing boats come and go. "If we could only have a fishing boat at Mols!" they sighed. "But we could never get together enough money to buy one."

Just then a ship came sailing in, which was towing something behind it on the end of a rope. The Mols men all wondered what this small thing could be. Some thought it was a whale, others said it must be a seal. Finally they saw that it was a small boat.

"It is surely the ship's child!" they cried. Then they said to one another, "We have not money enough to buy a big ship, but if we could buy the ship's child and then take good care of it, the small boat would finally grow to be a big ship like its mother."

So, they bargained with the ship's captain and bought the little boat and carried it back to Mols with them.

"We must put the ship's child near the beach where there is good green grass," they said. "And we must move it every day so that it will always have fresh food." But after a month the little boat had not grown at all.

Then they were anxious about the ship's child, and everyone had a different idea about what they should do to make it thrive and grow. They tried and tried, but nothing they did seemed to help at all. The little boat did not grow an inch!

Then the people from Mols were sorry that they had bought the ship's child. "It is a sickly little fellow and will never grow," they said, sadly.

"Perhaps it was taken away from its mother too soon," said one.

"Let us ask the captain to keep it with the mother a little longer," and they all agreed that this was the only thing to do, even if it cost them a good sum.

Then they carried the small boat to the captain and paid him to tie it to the ship again. When the ship sailed away, the waves rocked it back and forth and the small boat went bobbing along behind it.

"Look, see how lively the ship's child is! One can see how glad he is to be with his mother again!" cried the people of Mols. "We have certainly done the wise thing!"

The people from Mols were busy digging a well, but they were troubled because the more they dug, the higher grew the pile of earth beside the hole.

"What will we do with all this earth?" asked one.

"We must dig a hole in another place and put the dirt into it," said another.

This seemed a sound plan, and they at once began digging another hole.

Finally, one of the men said, "Yes, this is good, but where can we put the earth from the new hole we are digging?"

Then the wisest of the people of Mols answered, "We must dig a new hole, and we must make it so big that it will hold all the dirt from both of these smaller holes."

Once, some Mols men were on their way to the city with a cart full of dried fish. At the foot of a hill they stopped while their horse ate his fill of the long grass there.

Some bad fellows who lived on the hilltop, looked down and saw the cart full of dried fish and tried to think of a way to get it for themselves.

"We are not strong enough to drive off the men from Mols," they said. "We must think of some plan to make them run away and leave their cart."

So they got a wheel and bound straw around it; then they set fire to the straw. When the men from Mols saw the fire at the top of the hill, they said to one another, "What can that be, burning up there?"

"Perhaps it is the devil himself," said one.

"The devil cannot harm honest folk," said another. And although they were trembling with fright, the men began to sing:

"Honest hearts shall know no fear."

But at that moment the rascals up on the mountaintop gave the blazing wheel a push and it came rolling down the road.

When they saw the fire coming toward them, the Mols men sang:

> "Honest hearts shall know no fear,
> But I'm safer there than I am here."

And they ran off into the forest, leaving all their dried fish behind them.

One summer, when the grain was high in the fields, a stork came to Mols. The big bird walked up and down in the wheat, catching frogs, and everyone cried, "See now, the stork is tramping down our wheat!"

They talked of many ways to get rid of it, and finally decided that one of the farmers should go into the field and drive the stork away. But when he was starting out they all saw that the farmer with his large boots would certainly tramp down more grain than the stork.

So, they talked the matter over again, and one of the men from Mols said, "Let us carry the farmer into the field! He will not tramp on the grain if we all carry him."

This seemed an excellent plan, so they took the gate off its hinges, put the farmer on it and eight men carried him into the field so that he could frighten away the stork.

The people from Mols liked nothing better than pickled herring, but some years they could not afford to buy any because of high prices.

"If we could only raise pickled herring of our own, we would not have all this trouble and expense!" they said. "Live herring multiply in the sea; it ought to be the same with pickled herring. Let us buy a barrel of pickled herring and empty it into the village pond. Then each year we can fish out as many as we want of them."

So they bought a big barrel of pickled herring, and emptied it into the pond in the middle of the village.

The next year the men came and cast their nets in the pond, but not a single pickled herring could they catch. At last, after they had tried again and again, they brought up a fat eel in their net.

"Here is the thief!" cried the people of Mols. "This eel has eaten all of our pickled herring. It must be put to death at once!"

"How shall we put it to death?" asked one.

Some wanted to burn the eel, some wanted to hang it, and others said it should be whipped to death. Finally, an old man who had once been on the point of drowning and remembered how painful it was, said, "Let us carry the eel out to the open sea and drown it!"

"Let us do that without delay," said the people, and they climbed into a boat and rowed far out to sea.

The eel had been lying very still in the bottom of the boat, but when it was dropped into the sea the eel began to wriggle about, this way and that.

"The poor thing is twisting with pain," said the men from Mols. "But it deserves to suffer for having stolen our pickled herring."

Once, when the rumor went about that an enemy would march on Mols, the people made haste to hide everything they valued.

Their greatest treasure was the big Church bell,

and of course they wanted to put it in the safest place. It was a long and difficult work to take the bell down from the Church tower, and after that it was another task to find a hiding place for it.

At last they all agreed that the bell should be taken out in a boat and lowered to the bottom of the sea.

So they carried it down to the boat and rowed out a long way from shore. But when the bell had gone down with a big splash, the people began to be a little uneasy.

"The bell is well hidden from the enemy," they said, "but how will we find it again when the enemy is gone?"

One of the wisest of them took a knife from his pocket and cut a deep mark on the side of the boat.

"Now, we have marked the place where we threw the bell over! There will never be any question about that," they said, as they rowed back to the shore.

The Buried Treasure

FROM

PICTURE TALES FROM SCANDINAVIA

BY RUTH BRYAN OWEN

There was an estate in a northern land so large that all of the peasants for miles around, and even the keeper of the inn in the village, were tenants of the nobleman who owned it. One day he gave them orders to take all of the stones out of the fields when they were plowing. So, when the innkeeper ran his plow into a large stone deeply sunk in the earth, he called his farm boy to help move it away. They worked together, pushing and pulling at it until the stone finally moved from the place where it had been lying, and there they saw the lid of a chest which the stone had covered.

"There is certain to be money in that chest!" exclaimed the innkeeper, "but if I tell the lord of the manor about it he is sure to claim it for himself. I need every coin I can lay hands on for the repair of the inn. I must find a way to keep this treasure, if I can." So he offered to give his helper half of the money in the chest if he would tell no one about finding it.

At first the innkeeper thought he would not even tell his wife about it, but he was so pleased over his treasure that when they were going to bed that night he told his wife the whole story.

"Now we can repair the inn, and perhaps next summer we can build a fine new barn," he said, "but you must promise me never to tell anyone about the treasure. If you do, it will be bad for us both."

She promised that she would never speak about it to anyone, but the next day when a woman who came to the inn said that the place needed repairing, the innkeeper's wife could not keep silent any

longer. "There is something I would like to tell you," she said, "but alas! I promised my husband not to speak about it."

"You can certainly tell me," said the woman, "for I promise you that I will not speak of it to anybody else."

Then the wife said, "The inn will soon be repaired because my husband found a chest of money under a big stone in the field belonging to the lord of the manor. We might even build a new inn next summer, with all that gold."

"Of course, I will say nothing about it," the woman said, but on the way home she said to everyone she met, "It is splendid that we will have a fine new inn next summer," and when they asked, "Who will build it?" she answered, "The innkeeper who found a chest of gold in the field that belongs to the lord of the manor."

The news flew from mouth to mouth, and finally to the lord of the manor himself. He sent at once for the innkeeper, and asked, "Is it true what the people are saying, that you have found a chest of gold in my field? It seems that your wife has told about the finding of it."

"Perhaps she has told something of the sort,"

said the innkeeper, "but it means nothing. Sometimes my wife talks a little wildly and one should not take much notice of what she says. If you will only talk to her yourself you will understand just how matters are."

When the innkeeper returned home his wife was curious to know why her husband had been called by the lord of the manor.

"Oh, he told me the most terrible thing," said the innkeeper. "He says that the enemy are attacking our country and that there will be a battle around our inn tonight. It will be dreadful for you and for our treasure if the enemy should win, but I will lose my life rather than let them carry you away!"

"What shall we do! What shall we do!" cried the wife.

"I know what I will do," said the husband. "I will hide you and the treasure in our little smokehouse. Let happen to the inn what will, I will defend the smokehouse myself."

So that night the innkeeper put his wife and the money chest in the smokehouse. Then he went to the stable and led out the cows and goats and other stock and ran them around the smokehouse again and again, making as much noise as possible, and he took his old gun and put powder in it and fired it off many times.

The next morning everything was quiet, and the innkeeper opened the door of the smokehouse. "The battle is over," he said to his wife. "I shot many of the enemy and the rest have run away, taking their fallen comrades with them. Did you hear much of the fight?"

"I heard it all," his wife replied. "It was terrible . . . the banging of the cannon and the tramping of the soldiers. I was shaking all over with fear and did not dare to look out until the end of the battle."

When she had recovered from her fright, her husband said to her, "Shall we take a little trip today?"

"Is it safe to travel?" asked the wife anxiously.

"The enemy has left that part of the country now," replied the innkeeper. "We can travel in peace."

"Let us go then," said his wife, and they set off in their wagon.

When they reached the market town, his wife wanted to talk about the battle to the people whom

they met, but the innkeeper hurried her along so
that she had no chance to talk to anyone but him.

When they began their journey home his wife
fell asleep in the wagon. She had not slept at all
the night before and was half dead from weariness.

Just then they met in the road a woman who was
peddling bread, and when she asked the innkeeper
if he would not buy a loaf from her he replied, "I
will buy all the bread you have, but please be very
quiet, for my wife is sleeping." The woman was
very happy to sell all of her loaves to one buyer,
and the innkeeper took them and spread them on
the floor of the wagon, all around his wife.

After a little while he took a loaf and threw it at
her, and his wife woke up in a hurry.

"My dear husband," she cried, "What is happening? It looks to me as if it had been raining loaves
of bread."

"That is just what has happened!" replied her
husband. "There was a terrible storm while you
slept and the loaves of bread came raining down."

When they were nearing home they heard a
donkey braying on the other side of the hedge.
"What is that, my husband?" asked the wife. After
the battle of the smokehouse and the storm of

loaves of bread, she did not know what to expect next.

"I will tell you what it is," the innkeeper said, "but you must never tell anyone for the sake of the lord of the manor."

"I will tell no one, I promise you," the wife answered.

"The noise you hear is made by the lord of the manor himself," said her husband. "He borrowed money from the devil and did not repay him, and now the devil is giving him a sound beating. It is no wonder that he makes those cries!"

After that, when the donkey brayed, the good woman sighed and said, "Oh, our poor landlord! He is a very hard man but I do feel sorry for him!"

Some days later a message came that the lord of the manor wished to speak with the innkeeper's wife. She went at once and he said to her, "I hear that you have told that your husband found a chest full of money in my field."

"Yes, it is true," the wife said. "My husband did find a chest full of gold in your field."

"That is very interesting," replied the lord. "When did he find it?"

"I cannot tell you exactly," answered the woman,

"as I do not understand the calendar, but I know it was a few days before the great battle when the enemy were defeated between the inn and our smokehouse."

"What nonsense is this!" said the lord of the manor. "There has been no enemy attack on this land in my time or in yours."

"Surely you remember," said the woman. "You yourself told my husband that the enemy was coming and that there would be a big battle around our house. And you were right! There was a terrible noise all night, with all the running and shooting."

"Now," said the lord of the manor, losing his patience, "you must tell me when it was your husband found the chest of gold."

"Well, all I can say," answered the innkeeper's wife, "is that it was just before we had the storm when it rained loaves of bread."

"What are you saying!" cried the lord of the manor. "Again I ask you, what day did your husband find the chest of gold?" He thought that she must finally give a sensible answer to his question.

"I know how we can fix the day," said the woman. "My husband found the chest of gold a few days before the devil came and beat you because you did not pay him his due. You cried loudly enough and I am sure the devil was making it very uncomfortable for you."

"The poor woman's mind is wandering hopelessly," the landlord said to himself. "One must pay no attention to her strange fancies. But it is a sad thing for her poor husband, just the same."

So he sent her back to the inn and gave no more thought to the story of the buried treasure.

And all the repairs were made to the inn and a new barn was built next summer, which was the finest sight for many miles around.

The Talkative King

FROM

PICTURE TALES FROM INDIA

BY BERTA METZGER

Once there was an Indian King who talked
and talked so much that his ministers declared that
he talked from the moment he opened his eyes in
the morning until he closed them at night. Since
the King had no time to do anything but listen
to the music of his own voice, the business of the
once happy kingdom was at a standstill, as his ministers did not dare to interrupt him, for in those

ancient days it was dangerous to interrupt a king.

At last a great and noted sage came to the capital, and the King said, "I shall have this man for my adviser." And then he went right on talking. So the sage waited hoping that he would have an opportunity to give an object lesson to the King.

Now one day as the sage walked in the garden with the King and listened to his chitter-chatter, a tortoise fell from the heavens and crashed down at their feet. The King was so startled that he ceased his endless chitter-chatter and cried out in terror, "O Sage and Holy Man, what is the meaning of this strange happening? Why has this tortoise, a creature who dwells in water, fallen from the heavens and broken its shell at my feet?"

The sage held up his hands for silence, closed his eyes for a few moments and then said in a deep impressive voice, "Great King, it may be that the dead tortoise at your feet was but a little while ago dwelling in a pond in yonder snow-capped Himalayas. He was a very talkative tortoise and his chitter-chatter amused two wild geese who were very young. This morning the geese came to the pond where the tortoise lived and Spotted Wing said, 'Friend Tortoise, as winter draws near we must

now go to our home in the south. Will you not honor us with your company?'

"The eyes of the tortoise bulged with surprise, 'How can I go with you? I cannot fly!'

" 'We enjoy your conversation so much that we have planned to take you home with us,' replied Brown Wing.

" 'How? How?' cried Tortoise eagerly.

" 'If you can clamp your mouth over a stick and not open it once during the entire journey, we can carry you to our home in the south,' said Spotted Wing.

" 'I have always been called "The Talkative Tortoise," ' was the self-conscious reply. 'But if it is a matter of life or death, I can keep my mouth shut.'

" 'Then you will come with us?' cried the wild geese hopping about happily.

" 'I will! I will!' cried Tortoise.

"In a few moments Brown Wing brought a strong stick and said to Tortoise, 'Close your mouth over the middle of this, and we shall carry you between us. But remember, you must not open your mouth, no matter what happens.'

" 'I won't! I won't!' cried Tortoise, clamping his mouth over the middle of the stick.

"Then Brown Wing picked up one end of the stick in his beak, Spotted Wing picked up the other, and up they flew into the blue sky with The Talkative Tortoise between them. As they flew southward, Tortoise cocked his head to one side and looked down upon the green valleys and silver rivers, but not one word did he utter."

The sage shook his head sadly as he went on, "O Great King, as the wild geese approached your beautiful realm, they flew low in order that their guest might see the beauty of your royal palace, and the eyes of The Talkative Tortoise bulged with surprise at the splendor below him.

"Now some children were flying kites in one of the villages outside the palace walls. A small boy cried, 'Look! Look! There are three kites floating together in the sky!'

" 'Kites!' laughed his older brother. 'Those are two wild geese carrying a tortoise between them!'

" 'Wild geese carrying a tortoise! Whoever heard of such a thing?' cried the children clapping their hands and laughing.

"Their laughter made The Talkative Tortoise so angry that he forgot where he was and he was about to exclaim, 'What business is that of yours, you two-legged animals?' But when he opened his mouth to speak, O Great King, he fell and there he lies at your feet, a proof that he who does not learn to control his speech hurls himself into misfortune."

The King was silent for a moment and then he cried, "Has Heaven hurled this poor creature at my feet as an object lesson to me?"

"Be that true or not," replied the sage, "Misfortune always comes to those who talk too much."

The King pondered upon this, and from that day he ceased his endless chitter-chatter and once more the business of the kingdom was set in motion.

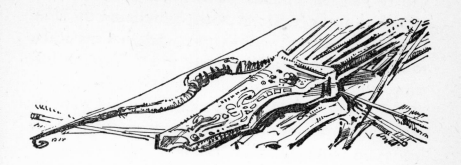

The Banyan Deer

FROM

PICTURE TALES FROM INDIA

BY BERTA METZGER

Once there was a beautiful deer of golden hue. His eyes were like round jewels; his horns had a silvery sheen; his mouth was as red as a bunch of scarlet cloth; his four hoofs were shiny as lacquer. He lived in the forest attended by a herd of five hundred, and was called King Banyan Deer. Near him dwelt the golden Branch Deer who was also attended by a herd of five hundred.

Now Brahmadatta, the King of Benares, was very fond of hunting and ate meat at every meal. Each day he called together his subjects, townsmen and countrymen alike, and went hunting. The people complained among themselves and said, "This King of ours stops all our work. Let us drive a herd of deer into his hunting park, and he can feed on them." So they went into the park, sowed grass for the deer to eat, supplied water for them to drink, and opened the gate. Then they went into the forest and happened to surround the herds of Banyan and Branch Deer. The people beat the trees, bushes, and ground with their sticks, rattled their swords and spears, and clanged their cymbals. Frightened by the great din, the deer ran out of hiding, and were driven into the hunting park.

The people closed the gate after the deer, and hastened to the King. "Sire," they said, "You put a stop to our work by going hunting every day. Therefore, we have driven two herds of deer into your hunting park. Henceforth feed on them."

Brahmadatta mounted his chariot and went to the park. He looked over the two herds and said, "Every day a deer shall be killed and brought to the palace, but do not on any account slay the two

golden kings of the deer."

Thereafter the King would sometimes shoot a deer with his bow and arrow, and sometimes the cook would. At sight of the hunter, the imprisoned animals would dash off trembling for their lives. After three or four arrows had been shot into the body of a deer, he would grow faint and sink down and be overtaken and slain. But many were pierced by arrows who were not slain, and many in terror hurled themselves against the fence and were grievously wounded.

Observing the suffering of the herds, Banyan Deer said to Branch Deer, "Friend, though our herds are imprisoned here and cannot escape death, at least they need not suffer as they do now. Let the deer go to the block in turns. One day let us sacrifice one deer from my herd, and the next day, one from yours. He upon whom the lots falls shall go to the place of execution and lie down with his head upon the block. In this way, the other deer will not be pierced by arrows and will not in terror hurl themselves against the fence."

All the deer agreed to this, and after that, he whose turn it was, went to the block and lay down with his head upon it.

One day the lot fell to a doe who had a little spotted fawn. She went to Branch Deer and said, "Sire, today is my turn to go to the block of execution. I have a nursling fawn who is as fair as the opening bud of the lotus. If I am taken from him now, he will die, and thus two of the herd will be sacrificed. I pray you, therefore, postpone my turn until my little one is old enough to forage for himself."

"Begone! I cannot make your turn another's!" cried Branch Deer indignantly. Then the doe went to Banyan Deer and made the same request.

The round jewel eyes of King Banyan filled with tears, and he said, "Go. Your turn shall be postponed." With grateful heart, she returned to her little spotted fawn, while Banyan Deer lay down with his head upon the block.

When the cook saw the golden animal, he cried, "Why, here's the King of the Deer! What can be the meaning of this?" and he ran to tell the King.

Brahmadatta mounted his chariot and galloped his horses all the way to the hunting park. He looked down upon the golden deer and cried, "My friend, King of Deer, did I not promise you your life? Why then are you lying here?"

Banyan Deer opened his round jewel eyes. "Sire, a doe came to me saying, 'Today is my turn to go to the block of execution. I have a nursling fawn who is as fair as the opening bud of the lotus. If I am taken from him now, he will die, and thus two of the herd will be sacrificed. I pray you, therefore, postpone my turn until my little one is old enough to forage for himself.' Therefore I have taken her doom upon me, and have laid my head upon the block. Think not that there is anything else behind this, my lord."

Brahmadatta cried, "My lord, the golden King of deer, never have I seen among men one so full of love and pity. Therefore I am pleased with you. Arise, for I spare your life and hers."

Still lying with his head upon the block, King Banyan asked, "Though two be spared, what shall the others do, O King of Men?"

"I spare their lives also, my lord," answered Brahmadatta.

"Sire, only the deer in your hunting park will thus be safe. What shall all other animals do?"

"I spare their lives also."

"But what of the birds of the air?"

"They too shall be spared."

"What of creatures who live in water?"

"I spare their lives also, my lord." Then King Brahmadatta went to the gate and opened it. The captive deer returned to the forest and henceforth they and all animals of the earth, all creatures of the air and all creatures of the sea, dwelt in safety in the kingdom of Brahmadatta.

Señor Coyote Settles a Quarrel

FROM

PICTURE TALES FROM MEXICO

BY DAN STORM

One morning when the sky was blue and the sun was bright and warm, the Rattlesnake crawled out of his den and lay down at the foot of the mountain and fell asleep. While he was fast asleep and dreaming there in the sun, a large boulder somehow loosened itself from the side of the mountain and came rolling to the bottom where it stopped and settled right on top of Señor Rattlesnake.

Of course the Snake woke out of his pleasant dreams and found himself in worse trouble than any bad dream. This great stone had him pinned to the ground. He lay there under the stone for perhaps an hour or more, twisting and squirming and grunting and stretching himself trying to escape, when he heard footsteps hopping down the canyon.

"Who could this be?" thought the Snake. "Certainly not one of my friends. I have none."

In a moment here came Señor Conejo (Mr. Rabbit).

"Help me! Help me! Brother Rabbit," called the Snake from under the rock. "Help me and I will see that you are well rewarded. Oh! My back, Brother Rabbit. My back! This rock is breaking it."

And the Rattlesnake began to cough, and catch his breath and groan as if he were near to death. Now the little Rabbit knew that the Snake was no friend of his, but he was such a kind-hearted animal that he hated to see even his worst enemy in such misery.

"Patience, Brother Rattlesnake," said the little Rabbit pleasantly. "I will get this rock off you somehow."

So the little Rabbit got a pole and put it under the stone and braced himself on the side of the mountain and lifted and heaved, and pushed and pried, until he finally rolled the heavy stone off the Rattlesnake.

"Now," said the Snake, "as to the reward that I was to give you."

"Oh, that will be all right," said the Rabbit.

"I think so, too," said the Snake with a grin which showed his forked tongue.

"What do you mean?" asked the Rabbit, becoming frightened.

"I mean," said the Snake, "that your reward will be that you will be my dinner."

"Oh, no!" said the Rabbit.

"Oh, yes. *Sí, sí, sí!*" said the Snake.

At this moment the Coyote appeared on the scene as if he had dropped out of the sky or just come from nowhere.

"What is going on here?" he asked.

The Snake and the Rabbit began talking at the same time.

"I helped the Snake," said the Rabbit. "I rolled this big stone off him, and now he wants to eat me as a reward."

"That is not true," said the Snake. "The Rabbit tried to roll the rock so that it would crush me worse than it had already."

"Wait a minute," said the Coyote. "One at a time. Let me think a minute."

So the Coyote took off his big sombrero and scratched his head with one hand and then held the hat in his other hand and scratched his head again.

"I tell you what we will do," he said at last. "Both of you go to the exact spot that you were in when the Rabbit came upon the scene. Then I can easily decide who is in the right after I have seen just how the situation was."

So the Coyote and the Rabbit pushed and shoved till they put the rock back on the Snake's back. Then at the Coyote's order, the Rabbit went up the canyon and came hopping back down to the rock and stopped.

"Is this the way it was, Brother Snake?" asked the Coyote.

"Yes, this is the way I was," said the Snake, squirming and making a face. "Get this rock off me right now."

"If that is the way you were," said the Coyote, "then that is the way you will stay. This is your reward for trying to eat Brother Conejo after he had treated you so kindly."

The War Between the Lion
and the Cricket

FROM

PICTURE TALES FROM MEXICO

By Dan Storm

The Lion, who is King of all the animals, one day met the Cricket and said to him with a loud laugh:

"You are much too small to be good for anything. What do you amount to in the world? It is a pity that you are not big and strong like me."

"Do you think so?" asked the Cricket. "If you think that I am good for nothing and can not fight, then let us fight a war, and we shall see if it is true that little people are not good soldiers."

When the Lion heard this brave speech from a creature so tiny, he threw back his great head and laughed so loudly that the earth trembled. But the little Cricket was not frightened and said,

"If you think what I said is so funny, then gather together all of your large creatures, and I will call together my army of little people and we will fight a war *mañana*." (That is the Spanish way of saying *tomorrow*.)

"Agreed!" roared King Lion. "Where shall we meet?"

"By the river," said the Cricket, "and I shall let you have the advantage of starting on top of the hill. My army will be down by the river, and at a given signal we will charge."

The next day, early in the morning, King Lion was standing at the top of the hill with his army of large animals. They had come from far and near and stood waiting eagerly for the moment of the battle.

At the foot of the hill, on the riverbank, stood the Cricket with his army of creatures no larger than himself. In his ranks were all the wasps, bees, bumblebees, hornets, and yellow jackets in the country, with their knives, spears, and swords sharpened and shining ready for combat. With this army was a large band of mosquitoes who with their constant humming made the music which kept the army of stinging insects in the mood for battle.

Up on the hill, King Lion glanced at the sun and said to the Burro, "It must be time for the battle. Go down there and ask the Cricket if he is ready. I am getting impatient for the fun. It is my duty to teach these little weaklings some respect for their King. The battle cannot amount to anything, but we shall have great sport."

So down the hill went the Burro and said to the Cricket, smiling, "Are you ready to fight, Brother Cricket?"

"Certainly," said the Cricket, "I am tired of waiting."

"Where are your men?" asked the Burro, looking all around. "I do not see any soldiers anywhere."

"In here they are," the Cricket said, opening a door in the clay bank of the river.

The Burro looked inside and there were the wasp, bees, bumblebees, hornets, yellow jackets, and musical mosquitoes, all lined up row and row in the cave, one behind the other.

"There are plenty of them," said the Burro, "and they are all about the same size, as soldiers should be; but they cannot harm anyone. They are not big and strong."

"No," said the Cricket, "it is true. They are not very large; but they are very brave."

"All right, then," said the Burro, "send one of them out here and let us see what he can do."

So the Cricket called to one of his hornets who came zooming out of the cave and stung the Burro right on the very end of his nose. The Burro reared up on his hind legs and with a loud bray of pain and surprise, turned and ran up the hill.

He called the Lion aside and said to him quietly, so the other soldiers of the King's army could not hear:

"Listen. You will not believe this, but that Cricket sent one of his men out; he knifed me right here on the nose, and it is still hurting. If all your army knew how fierce these little creatures are, not one of your soldiers would go into battle for you. I, for one, do not want to go against them."

The Lion thought a moment and then said, "It

is true that I find it hard to believe what you say. But it may be that he has only one or two of these little demons who stab so viciously. This is what we will do: we will send all the other animals in the front, while you and I will bring up the rear. What we do depends upon how those in front come out in the first few blows of the battle."

The Burro agreed to the King's plan, but none too willingly. The Lion roared down to the Cricket that he was ready to fight. So down the hill charged the thundering army of big animals: the Horse, the Bear, the Ox, the Fox, the Coyote, *Lobo* the wolf, the Panther, the Armadillo, *Javalina* the wild pig, and all the others. Hardly had the King's proud and eager army reached the clay bank of the river when the little Cricket swung open the door in the bank and out swarmed his army in a great black cloud, so dark that the sun was nearly hidden. This sudden darkness threw the army of giant animals into helpless confusion, so that they began milling and stumbling about, running into each other and falling down. Before they could recover, the midget army dived down in one cloud and began attacking the big tooth-and-claw and hoof-and-horn animals from every direction with their sharp swords, spears, knives and lances. And all the while the mosquito band kept playing its most stirring battle tune. The King's men, so brave just a moment ago, now roared and yelled with pain and surprise, crying out:

"Where are they? Where are they!"

"If you cannot see us, then perhaps you can feel us," chirped the Cricket.

The air was filled with dust from the milling animal feet, and nothing could be heard but all kinds of beast voices yelling and bellowing and snorting. Some jumped high into the air while others fell to the ground and rolled over and over in the dirt, tripping those who were trying to stand up or climb out of the crowd to escape. The Lion and the Burro did not escape their share of the punishment. In fact, the Cricket had sent a special band of his best hornets and yellow jackets to take care of the King and his right-hand man. So these two fellows could be heard plainly above the din.

All at once there was a general movement in the direction of the river; and the King's army went running and climbing over each other, racing to the stream, and jumped off the bank into the water. *Splash! Splash! Splash! Splash!* Those who were

able, swam under the water downstream and nearly drowned themselves rather than face the deadly little insects. Every time an animal nose appeared above the water there would be a Cricket soldier there with his weapon ready.

The Lion, coughing and gagging and swatting the air with his paws, called to the Cricket, "I surrender! I surrender!" So the little Cricket gave the command to stop attacking. And the Lion climbed out on the bank dripping wet and very humble. Holding out his tremendous paw to the little Cricket, he said:

"Shake my hand, little fellow. Your people are very small but very brave. I know now that one does not have to be big in order to fight."

All this happened a long, long time ago. But from that day to this, the big people of the Lion's army and the little creatures of the Cricket's army have been the best of friends.

The Little Bucket

FROM

PICTURE TALES FROM THE ITALIAN

By FLORENCE BOTSFORD

Once there was a mother who had two little daughters, one was very, very good and the other was very, very naughty. One day the mother said to the naughty little girl, "Will you please fetch a bucket of water?"

The naughty little girl answered, "No, I won't."

Then the good little girl said, *"I* will get the water for you, dear Mother," and she started off to the well in the deep woods.

The naughty little girl stuck out her tongue at her sister and screamed at the top of her voice:

"Goody, goody, sniffle nose,
  Knock your head and stub your toes."

The good little girl walked so swiftly that she caught her toe on the well curb and the bucket went bang, bang, bang, right down to the bottom. She sat down and cried, "Now what shall I do? I have lost the bucket! Oh, what will Mother say!"

She looked down into the well and saw the bucket floating around on the water, so she climbed down very carefully, but when she got to the water the bucket was gone. She sat down again and cried until a fish stuck out its head and said, "Little girl, if you don't stop crying you will make the water salt as brine and I cannot live in salt water."

"I hope you will excuse me," said the little girl, "but I have lost my bucket."

"Stop crying," said the fish, "and knock upon that white door and you will find your bucket."

When the good little girl knocked on the white door it flew open and within stood a beautiful lady

in a glittering green dress who asked, "What do you want?"

"I have come to find my bucket," said the little girl.

"You must clean my house and make the fire and cook my supper and if you do these things very well you may have your bucket."

So the good little girl scrubbed and cleaned until her back ached and she lighted the fire and made the house nice and warm and cooked a fine supper. The beautiful lady in the green dress said:

"Here is the bucket, but do not look inside until you get home." And she kissed the good little girl on the forehead.

The good little girl hurried back to her mother and told what had happened and when they looked in the bucket it was filled with pearls and precious stones and on the forehead of the good little girl there shone a bright diamond.

Now the naughty little girl thought *she* would get a bucket full of treasures also, so she snatched the bucket and ran to the well in the deep woods. The good little girl waved her hand to her sister and said:

"Sister mine, sweet sister fair,
  May you find the jewels rare."

The naughty little girl climbed down into the well. When she saw the fish swimming around she said, "Where is the door to the treasure room?"

And the fish answered, "All fish are deaf; we cannot hear you."

"I'll make you hear," said the naughty little girl and she kicked at the fish and made such a noise that suddenly the white door opened and the beautiful lady in the glittering green dress said sternly, "What do you want?"

"I have come to fill my bucket with jewels. Tell me where they are."

"If you clean my house I will give you your reward."

So the naughty little girl swept all the dust under the stove and put some cold food on the table and did not even try to build a fire. Then she said to the beautiful lady in the glittering green dress, "Quick, I want my bucket of jewels." And she snatched it and hurried home, and when they opened the bucket it was full of scorpions and toads and on her forehead lay a stone.

Then the naughty little girl was sorry that she had not tried to be good like her sister.

The Eagle and the Owl

FROM

PICTURE TALES FROM THE ITALIAN

By Florence Botsford

There was once an eagle who was the King of all birds. He flew over mountains and valleys looking for little birds to eat.

One day he saw in the top of a tall pine tree the nest of a Mother Owl and in the nest were four eggs.

King Eagle stopped beside the nest and the Mother Owl said politely, "Good morning, King

Eagle, I hope you are not very hungry?"

"Yes, I am!" said King Eagle. "And I am going to eat up your owlets just as soon as they are hatched."

"Oh, King Eagle!" said the Mother Owl, "if you will not eat my owlets I promise that ever after I will fly only at night, and I will eat the snakes and scorpions and leave the birds and mice for you, who fly by day."

"Very well," said King Eagle, "I promise not to eat your owlets. But how will I know them from other birds?"

"Oh, surely, you will know them because they will be the most beautiful birds in the world," said the Mother Owl.

King Eagle flew over the mountains searching for food with his sharp eyes. Soon he saw a nest in the top of a tall pine tree where four tiny white birds were fast asleep. He screamed for joy and rushed down to eat them up. But when he came to the nest the baby birds said, "Chee-eep! Chee-eep!" and looked so sweet that King Eagle said to himself, "These must be Mother Owl's babies. I will not eat them."

Soon he saw another nest in the top of a tall tree

and he swooped down and there, in the nest, were four of the ugliest little birds he had ever seen and they were screeching, "To-whoo! To-whoo! To-whoo!"

"Ha!" said King Eagle. "These ugly birds can not belong to Mother Owl." And he gobbled them up.

Just then Mother Owl flew down to her nest and began to cry, "To-whit, To-whoo! To-whit, To-whoo! To-whit! To-whoo-oo-O-O-OO! King Eagle, you have broken your promise. You have eaten up my owlets! Oh, what shall I do?"

"Excuse me!" said King Eagle. "You told me that your owlets were the most beautiful birds in the world—and those I ate were the ugliest little birds I have ever seen."

"To-whit! To-whoo! To-whit, To-shoo-oo-O-O-OO!" cried Mother Owl. "You are the King of Birds and you have not yet learned that *every* mother thinks her own children the most beautiful in the world!"

Little Cricket

FROM

PICTURE TALES FROM THE FRENCH

By Simone Chamoud

Once upon a time there lived a man who had never grown like other people, and was no taller than a small child. When he spoke his voice sounded like the chirping of a cricket and for this reason everyone who knew him called him "Little Cricket." As he was frail and weak, no one wanted to hire him, and so he had to live on the skimmed milk which some kind farmers' wives saved for him.

Everywhere he went he heard people boast of the good food they ate, and as he had nothing to do all day, Little Cricket's mind was always filled with thoughts of food, and at night he used to dream of big juicy roasts and rich creamy puddings.

One day he could stand it no longer, and setting his wits to work, he thought of a scheme whereby he would at least eat a few good meals while he was still on earth.

"If I go far from here, where no one knows me, and pretend that I am a great wizard," he said to himself, "I may find some one who will need my services. But before undertaking anything, I shall insist on having three days of deep thinking and three hearty meals along with them."

So he left his village, and after traveling for a long time, he arrived at the palace of the Queen of the Netherlands. It happened that the day before, the Queen had lost a valuable diamond ring to which she had been greatly attached. When Little Cricket offered to find it, he was brought before the Queen's counselor. "A wizard, eh!" the counselor sniffed. "Well, then, you must know that Her Majesty the Queen has lost her diamond ring. If you find it, you shall be rewarded; but if you fail, you will *hang!*"

This was more than Little Cricket had bargained for, but it was too late now to withdraw. Besides anything was better than a future on skimmed milk, so he decided to take the chance.

"I'll find the ring," he promised. "That won't be very difficult. But I have to think deeply for three whole days, and must eat three good meals of soup, roast ham, dessert and coffee; one dinner a day. After I have had the third, I assure you that I'll have Her Majesty's ring."

"Very well; but see that you find it," warned the counselor.

That day Little Cricket was served with the sort of dinner of which he used to dream. A servant saw to it that he lacked nothing. Indeed, afraid he would wake up and find himself in his old bed, Little Cricket ate for all he was worth, until at last he fell asleep in his chair, mumbling drowsily, "Well, that's one I've got hold of."

The following day another dinner was brought to him—by a different servant this time—and Little Cricket found it even more delicious than the first.

When he had finally eaten to his heart's content, he murmured, "Ah, that's the second one now," and dropped off to sleep on the spot.

The third day he feasted again. Now, although Little Cricket thought it somewhat strange that he was waited upon by yet another servant, the dinner was so excellent that it occupied all his mind and he did not give the matter a second thought. He ate heartily and drank well. As he swallowed the last mouthful, he said to himself, "Well, my lad, you've had your hands on all three!"

The three servants who had waited upon him, and who were listening outside the door, heard what he said and rushed into the room. They fell on their knees before him and cried:

"Have mercy on us, Master Wizard. It is no use hiding anything from you; we stole the ring. But please help us, Master; have pity on us or we shall hang."

Little Cricket almost fell out of his chair when he heard this. It dawned upon him that the thieves had thought he meant *them*, instead of the meals, when he had said, "Now you've laid your hands on all three."

"Of course," he asserted, "I knew that you three

had stolen the ring, and you would have hung to-morrow. But I'm not a bad sort, and since you have confessed, I will help you. Give me the ring and go to the poultry yard and bring me back a goose that can be easily distinguished from the rest."

The three knaves, only too glad to be relieved of the ring, gave it to Little Cricket and brought him a goose with black tail feathers. Cricket made the goose swallow the ring, and returned the bird to the poultry yard. Then he sent a message to the Queen, asking to see her at once.

"Your Majesty," he said, when he was in her presence, "were you not in the royal poultry yard last week?"

"Yes, my friend, I was there."

"You dropped your ring there, Your Majesty, and a goose swallowed it."

"Can it be possible!"

"It is a fact, Your Majesty, and I can show you the goose that swallowed it."

The Queen's court, curious as to what was about to happen, trailed behind the Queen and Little Cricket. At the poultry yard the dwarf ordered that all the geese be led past him. When the goose with the black tail feathers waddled by, Little Cricket told a servant to catch it and kill it. In its stomach lay the ring, to the Queen's great joy.

"You really are a great wizard!" she exclaimed. "If you wish, you may stay at the palace here and feast every day. And when you decide to leave, I will give you a purse of gold."

"You are very kind, Your Majesty, and I thank you for your hospitality, which I gratefully accept."

So Little Cricket remained at the palace and lived well. But one fine day, the King of the Netherlands returned from the wars and heard the story of the famous wizard.

"I have not much faith in your wizard," he grumbled to the Queen. "I do not want him to be leading a gay life here at my expense, just because he happened once to guess right. I shall try him out. If he is as good as you say, he shall have his purse of gold, but if he's been deceiving you, he shall hang."

As he spoke, the King caught hold of a house cricket which he had spied on the hearthstone. He hid the insect between two silver plates, and sent for the little man.

"If you really are a wizard," the King thundered, "you will tell me at once what is hidden between these plates. If you cannot, you shall hang."

"Alas, alas, poor Little Cricket," wailed the supposed wizard, "this time you are caught."

"Extraordinary!" exclaimed the King. "The Queen was right—you *are* a great wizard. You guessed absolutely right."

The King was so pleased that he gave Little Cricket a large purse filled with gold. And as for Little Cricket, he was so proud of himself for having succeeded so well as a wizard, that he returned to his native village, where he lived a happy life for the rest of his days.

Jan and Jaantje

FROM

PICTURE TALES FROM HOLLAND

By Johan Hart

Once upon a time a young peasant by the name of Jan Hoogevink, married a girl called Jaantje. Jan was not very bright, but Jaantje was the biggest ninny that ever lived.

Now, every Monday morning Jan went to market in town to sell some of the things he grew on his farm. One day, after he had saved enough money, he bought a pig. When he got home, Jan said to his wife:

"Give this pig plenty of good fodder, Jaantje, and it will fatten up quickly. Then when it is plump enough, we'll kill it and have a fine lot of pork."

"Well and good, Jan," agreed Jaantje. "I will give it a big bowl of milk mixed with bran every morning."

And, indeed, as Jaantje took such good care of the pig, it grew fat in no time. Then Jan fetched the butcher, who slaughtered the pig and cut it up into twelve large chunks. Jan salted the meat and put the pieces in the larder down in the cellar.

His mouth watered for a piece then and there, but he went firmly upstairs and said to his wife:

"Jaantje, be sparing with this meat, now, and don't put too big pieces in the soup. If we are careful with it, there are enough pieces for January, February, March, April, May, June, July, August, September, October, November and December."

"As you say, Jan," said Jaantje readily.

The next morning Jan went off to plow his fields. A moment later a tramp, who had overheard the conversation between the two the day before, poked his head in the kitchen, and said:

"Please, *Vrouw Boer,* could you give poor January something to eat?"

"Oh, are you January?" asked Jaantje. "Yes, indeed, I have something for you." And down the cellar she went, bringing back in her hand a big chunk of pork.

"We have just slaughtered our pig," she explained, "and Jan told me to save some for you. Here is the piece he said we should keep for January."

The tramp took the pork, and thanking Jaantje very politely, went his way.

The following day he appeared begging at Jaantje's door again, this time in different tatters.

"And what is *your* name?" asked Jaantje.

"I am February, *Vrouw Boer.*"

"Very well, February," said Jaantje, bringing up the second piece of pork from the cellar, "here is your piece."

"Many thanks, good Vrouw!" shouted the tramp, as he disappeared again. But he returned the next day, and the next, and the next, until he had called himself each and every one of the names of the months in the year, and in that manner secured for himself the whole of poor Jan's precious pig.

One cold day, not long after the tramp had taken the last piece of pork, Jan came into the house, rubbing his hands excitedly, and called out to his wife:

"A good plate of soup and pork would go well today, Jaantje! What do you say we begin on one of the big pieces of our pork? You'd better put the kettle on the fire and start the soup, while I run down to the cellar."

"Oh, but there is no pork left, Jan!" replied Jaantje.

"What!" shouted Jan. "What has happened to it?"

"Why, you told me yourself to keep some for January, February, March, April, May, June, July, August, September, October, November, and December. Didn't you?"

"Yes," blurted Jan, "but——"

"Well, then," Jaantje explained, "they've all been here during the past fortnight, and I gave them the pieces you told me to keep for them."

"They! Them! What are you talking about?" gasped Jan. "Why, you goose, that wasn't what I meant at all! But it's no use trying to explain it to you. . . . You are too silly even to live with!"

Saying this, Jan grabbed his cap, which was hanging on a nail near the chimney corner, and marched out, banging the door behind him.

And that was the last poor, stupid Jaantje ever saw of him!

The Magic Cap

FROM

PICTURE TALES FROM HOLLAND

By Johan Hart

There was once a farmer of whom his neighbors used to say that he had no more wits than he was born with, which were not very many. Although it was easy to get the best of him, he was fortunate in having for a wife a woman who was very smart and sharp as a needle. Hence Willem, as he was called, left all of the thinking to his wife and did whatever she told him to do.

One bright, sunny morning she said, "Willem, put on a clean smock and your Sunday clogs and take the cow with you to sell at the market. She is very fat and looks well; so you should get at least a hundred guilders for her."

So to the market went the farmer, pulling his cow behind him.

As he passed a certain inn, three ne'er-do-wells were standing in the doorway.

"There goes Willem, the simpleton," remarked one of them. "It should be easy enough to fool him."

The three put their heads together for an instant and straight away agreed on a plan to get Willem's cow for little money. Then they took a short cut across the fields and stood here and there along the road where Willem would pass.

As the farmer came towards him, the first scamp called out:

"Hi, Farmer, are you taking that donkey to market?"

"That is not a donkey; that is a cow," answered Willem.

"Ho, ho! Ha, ha! What kind of a farmer are you to think it is a cow?" And shaking with laughter, the scoundrel walked on.

Shortly afterwards Willem met the second rogue, who said:

"Why don't you ride that donkey instead of pulling him, Farmer?"

"That is not a donkey; that is a cow," replied Willem again.

"A cow? Why, Farmer, you must be blind to take that animal for a cow!" And the second scoundrel walked on.

Poor Willem turned around and looked at his cow doubtfully. Had he taken the wrong animal out of the stable? But no, there could be no mistake—this *was* their cow—the one his wife had told him to take to market. Still his wife might be wrong too—they might both be mistaken, and perhaps he *was* leading a donkey, instead of a cow, to market.

Then he met the third scamp. "Good morning, Farmer. Is your donkey for sale?"

There! thought Willem. That was the third person to talk about a *donkey;* he and his wife *must* be wrong.

"Yes," he finally replied, "I am taking this donkey to market."

"In that case," said the other, "I will buy it from you for twenty guilders."

Now, twenty guilders was a good price for a donkey, so Willem agreed and went back to his farm, well satisfied that he had made a good sale.

When he got home his wife called him all kinds of an idiot, until he hung his head in shame. But she knew that it was not altogether his fault that he had gotten the worst of a bad bargain, so she put on her thinking cap and tried to find a way to get even with the three ne'er-do-wells.

Well, just before the next market day, the farmer's wife arranged to go to town and lay a trap for the three tramps. On market day itself she gave the farmer an old cap and told him exactly what he was to do with it.

As Willem was trudging along the road that led to town, he met the three ne'er-do-wells, who stopped to crow over the trick they had played on him.

"Oh, let bygones be bygones," said the farmer good-naturedly. "I have some money to spend to-day. Will you come and have a glass of wine with me?"

They gladly accepted and followed him to an inn.

After they had all refreshed themselves, the farmer looked at the innkeeper and twirling his cap three times upon the forefinger of his right hand, asked, "Everything is paid for, is it not?"

"Yes, everything is paid for," the innkeeper repeated, as the farmer walked out, followed by his fair-weather friends.

As they were passing the next inn, Willem stopped and said aloud, as though talking to himself:

"It should work here, too," and asking the ne'er-do-wells to join him in another drink, he went inside. And again after they had had their fill, Willem spun his cap around his finger and walked out without paying a cent.

The rogues' eyes were by now fairly popping out of their heads, but no one spoke a word. When they came to the third inn, the farmer said, "Let's have dinner here; it won't cost a thing."

So the four went in and ordered a good dinner. When everyone had eaten and drunk his fill, the farmer picked up his cap and twirled it around his finger again, and lo and behold! once more the innkeeper said everything had been paid for.

By that time the three ne're-do-wells could no

longer hold back their curiosity and began question-
ing Willem. They wanted to know how he could
eat and drink in every inn he went to without paying for anything.

The farmer told them that the secret lay in the
cap. It was a magic cap, he said.

"How much do you want for your cap?" the first
one asked. "I'll give you fifty guilders for it!" he
added eagerly.

"I will give you eighty!" the second one cried.

"One hundred!" shouted the third, who was the
greediest of all and whose mouth watered when he
thought of all the good food and wine he would
get if he had the cap in his possession.

"Sold!" said Willem.

The farmer ran all the way home with the hundred guilders in his hand; and how his wife chuck-
led when he gave her the money! "That's eighty
guilders for our loss in the sale of the cow; ten
guilders for the food and wine you and your fine
friends feasted upon, which I paid for in advance
yesterday, when I went to town; and ten guilders
to teach those rascals a lesson," she counted, as she
put the money in an old stocking and hid it on one
of the low wooden beams above her head.

How the Camel Got His Proud Look

FROM

PICTURE TALES FROM THE CHINESE

By Berta Metzger

When the Lord of Heaven created the camel he looked very much like other animals. One day he started to walk out upon the desert and found that his feet sank into the sand, and he made little progress. So he returned to the Lord of Heaven and complained, "I long to live upon the beautiful desert, but my four small feet sink down into the sand like sticks. I pray you, make them so they will carry me over the desert."

So the Lord of Heaven reshaped the camel's feet and made them large and flat. Then the camel returned to the desert and *plop-plopped* over the sand with the greatest ease. He walked proudly, for he was much pleased with himself. He had not gone far, however, when he was overcome with hunger and thirst. He turned round, and *plop-plopped* back again. He went to the Lord of Heaven a second time and said:

"My feet carry me over the desert with the greatest ease. But I can go only a short distance when I am overcome with hunger and thirst. I pray you, change my body so I can carry enough food and drink for many days."

The Lord of Heaven laughed good-naturedly. Then he reshaped the camel again, and back he went to the desert. He found that he could carry food and drink for many days. But whenever he met other animals they stood about and laughed and laughed, and cried out:

"See his humps and his lumps, and his pancake feet!"

This hurt the pride of the camel. He hastened back to the Lord of Heaven a third time, and complained:

"Wherever I go the other animals stand about and laugh and cry, 'See his humps, and his lumps, and his pancake feet!' I pray you, change me back to the form I had at first."

The Lord of Heaven replied, "That, even I, cannot do."

Then the camel went away, and thought and thought. At last he returned for the fourth time to the Lord of Heaven, and said, "I ask but one thing more. Give me a superior look. Then I shall gaze down upon the other animals of your creation and make them believe they are inferior to me."

The Lord of Heaven laughed heartily. He gave the camel's chin an upward shove. Then he pushed the nose back a trifle so that the camel looked as if he smelled something most unpleasant. Then off into the desert the camel *plop-plopped* on his large pancake feet. He carried his humps and his lumps proudly.

Soon he met other animals. He sniffed and looked down his nose at them with large and glassy eyes. And to this day, all animals, including men, shrink before the disdainful look of the camel.

The Golden Boat

FROM

PICTURE TALES FROM THE CHINESE

BY BERTA METZGER

Once there was a youth who lived with his aunt. She was a very mean and dishonest woman. The youth was always such a good boy that his aunt thought him stupid. She wanted to make him leave home and never return. Every day she sent him to a swamp to catch frogs, and told him not to come back until his basket was full. But his basket always was full, so she found no excuse for driving him away.

One morning as he went to the swamp to catch frogs, he saw a bag of money lying beside the path. He did not know whose it was, so he sat down and watched over it. He hoped that the owner would return for it. Toward evening he saw a man looking here and there along the path. "Have you lost anything?" asked the boy.

"Yes, a bag of money," said the man, who looked very worried.

"I found it, and here it is," said the youth.

The man was so happy to get all his money back that he said, "I will give you half of this."

The youth replied, "I do not want a reward. I have done only my duty."

When he returned home, his aunt saw his empty basket. She thought to herself, "Now I have an excuse for driving this stupid boy from home." So she cried out, "How dare you return with an empty basket?"

The boy told her what had happened. "You are even more stupid than I thought," she shrieked at him. "Take your basket and stick, and go. And don't ever let me see your face again!" And she drove him away.

It was the night of the Moon Festival, and the moon was big and bright. As the youth walked along he wondered where he would go. He looked up at the full moon and recalled what he had often heard. That on the night of the Moon Festival, he who looks long at the moon may see some beautiful object floating down toward him. And that object always brings good luck. The youth gazed and gazed at the heavenly mirror. At last he saw a tiny golden boat floating down on a silver moonbeam. Little people were rowing the boat. Some were playing musical instruments; some were singing; some were dancing.

With a shout of joy the youth held out his basket and cried, "Heavenly boat! Heavenly boat! Drop into my basket!"

One of the musicians bowed and said, "Because you are so kind and so honest, we have come to help you." Then he went into the golden boat, and all the other little people followed him.

The door closed behind them, and the golden boat became smaller and smaller and fell into the basket.

The happy youth walked on with his treasure. At last he came to the city of the Emperor. Here he heard of a princess who was both beautiful and good. Hoping to catch sight of her, he went to the palace and found work as a servant.

Sometimes when he was tired he took the little boat from the treasure bag which hung from his waist and looked at it. Sometimes he cried out, "Heavenly ones, heavenly ones, come and play for me!" Then the tiny beings stepped out upon the deck and played, sang, and danced for him.

The Emperor heard of the golden boat. He commanded that the owner bring it to him. When the youth stood before the dragon throne, he held the tiny boat in his two hands and cried, "Heavenly ones, heavenly ones, come and play for me."

Out stepped the little people and began to entertain the Emperor. He was delighted and longed to have it for his own. He promised the youth his daughter in marriage if he would give him the golden boat. The youth gave it to him, but the Emperor had no thought of carrying out his promise. That wicked man had the youth taken to the house of the Demon with the Red Face and the Demon with the Green Face. The Emperor well knew that no man had ever spent a night in that house, and lived.

At midnight the Demon with the Red Face and

the Demon with the Green Face burst into the house. Their long noses twitched as they sniffed about in the dark. Red Face cried, "Some one has dared to enter our house!"

"Yes! And here he is!" cried Green Face, who leaned over the youth who was sleeping quietly in the moonlight with a happy smile upon his face.

Red Face gasped and cried, "A blue lotus youth. How beautiful he is!"

"He must be from heaven!" murmured Green Face.

The youth woke and opened his eyes. He smiled up at the two demons and asked, "Have you come at the command of the Emperor?"

They shook their heads. Green Face asked, "Are you a being of heaven or of earth?"

The youth smiled and answered, "I am of earth."

"Do you fear me?" shouted Green Face.

"Do you fear me?" shouted Red Face.

The youth looked puzzled and asked, "Fear you? Why should I fear you? Do you fear me?"

At this the demons gasped with surprise. They looked at each other, and burst into laughter that made the roof tiles dance. At last Green Face said, "Blue Lotus Youth, we will give this house to you.

We will show you where all our treasures are hidden. They, too, shall be yours."

The next morning when the officers of the Emperor came to the house of the Demon of the Red Face and the Demon of the Green Face, they expected to find the youth dead. Imagine their surprise when he came to meet them clad in beautiful embroidered robes. He said, "Send your servants here. I have gifts which I wish to take to the palace."

Blue Lotus Youth took some of the treasures to the Emperor, who was surprised, for they were more precious than anything in the palace. He saw that the youth was so good and honest that he did not suspect him of evil. Even the demons had been kind to him. This filled the Emperor with shame, and he welcomed the youth to the palace and gave him for his wife the Princess who was both beautiful and good.

Happy indeed were the young bride and groom. And the goodness of the youth shone like a white light through the lantern of his face. Little by little the cruelty and dishonesty of the Emperor changed to kindness and honesty. Thus, all unknowing, Blue Lotus Youth became a great power for good in the Empire.

One day the youth said to the Princess who was still his wife, "I shall send to my aunt enough money so that she may live in comfort all her life." And with the bag of money, he sent a note thanking her for her kindness in sending him forth into the world, and thus helping him to find happiness.

The Peach Boy

FROM

PICTURE TALES FROM THE JAPANESE

By Chiyono Sugimoto

In the olden time there was an old man and an old woman who lived on the edge of a forest. They were very poor, but they were industrious and contented, and would have been the happiest couple in the world only that the little thatched hut had always been empty of children's voices.

One morning the old man went to the mountain to gather dry branches and the old woman went to the brook to wash her clothes. As she placed her wooden tub at the edge of the water, she listened a moment to the twittering of the forest birds, then gazed down at the pebbly bottom of the brook and watched the tiny fish that darted in and out among the ripples.

"Ai," she sighed. "The birds are whispering to their young and the fish are teaching their little ones to swim, but my arms have withered without having known the blessed burden of a babe."

And then something happened. Far in the distance, she saw a big peach on the water bobbing up and down, and rolling over and over as it came sailing along in the middle of the stream.

"Maa! Maa!" cried the old woman. "The snow is on my hair but never have my eyes beheld such a peach as this. It will furnish a delicious feast for my good husband." And she looked for a long pole. There was none near, and in fear of losing the prize she eagerly leaned forward, clapping her hands and singing in her quavery voice:

> "Come!
> The far-away waters are salty.
> The stream near the shore is sweet.
> Come!"

Three times she sang this. The peach seemed to understand, for it floated nearer and nearer until it bobbed up beneath her hand, and she rolled it into her wooden tub. Then she hurried home as fast as her aged feet could carry her and waited with impatient heart for her husband's return. At last she saw him toiling down the mountain path with his back heavily piled with dry branches. She ran to meet him.

"Old man, old man, make haste," she called happily. "I have something wonderful to show you."

"Maa! Maa!" muttered the old man as he backed up against the hut to rest his burden while he loosened the rope. "It must be something extraordinary that you make such a noise. Women chatter like sparrows." But he hurried to wash his feet in the water the old woman brought him, then stepping up to the floor, he gazed with astonishment at the huge peach in the tub.

While the old woman eagerly told how it was brought by the waves of the stream, he shook his head from side to side and drew in his breath with long "ah—" of wonder. Then she brought the big fish knife, and he was lifting it to cut the peach when there sounded a soft smothered voice.

"Old man! Old man! Wait!" it called.

The next moment the peach suddenly opened. There was no stone in the center, but sitting cross-legged in its place was a smiling little boy.

The old couple were so astonished that they stood back, blinking their eyes and saying not a word.

The child stepped out to the floor.

"Honorable Father and Mother," he said, "the gods have sent me to be your son."

With many bows and indrawn breaths of gratitude and joy the heavenly son was received. They called the child Momotaro—Peach Boy—and brought him up with loving care. As the years passed he grew so strong and willing that the old man spent his time nodding by the firebox, while his son carried the brush from the mountain and did the work of their tiny rice field.

The day Momotaro was fifteen years old, he came to his father and bowed low.

"Honorable Father," he said, "during the years you have cared for me your kindness has been higher than the mountain where you gather brush, and deeper than the stream where my mother washes her clothes. I have no words to thank you.

But now I beg your permission to leave."

"Alas! Alas!" cried the troubled father, "I cannot refuse the request of so dutiful a son. But why do you wish to leave me?"

"Honorable Father, all the people of the Land of the Rising Sun know of the fearful demons green and red. They ruin our rice fields, kill our people, and steal our temple treasures. I want to go to the Demon Island and revenge the wrongs of our land. I ask your permission."

The father did not delay his reply an instant.

"Momotaro, my god-sent son," he said, "although so young, you are brave. Go and conquer the demons green and red."

The next day, the old man brought an ancient sword encased in its sheath of fur, and a black war fan which he decorated with the emblem of a peach. The old woman pounded dough and made a bag of rice dumplings as provision for the journey. Then Momotaro started. As he marched bravely down the hill, the old woman hid her wet eyes behind her sleeve, but the old man waved his high-lifted hand.

"Momotaro of the Land of the Rising Sun," he shouted, "courage leads to victory! Banzai!"

The day was bright and clear. The youth journeyed until he came to a lonely mountain road, when suddenly a large dog sprang out from the shadow of a rock.

"Bow-wow! Bow-wow!" he fiercely barked. "Give me a rice dumpling or I'll tear you to pieces!"

Momotaro laughed.

"Be silent! I am Momotaro on my way to conquer the demons green and red."

The dog immediately crouched to the ground in a deep bow.

"Most honorable Momotaro, all Dogland knows of your brave journey. I beg you to permit me to go with you."

"I consent. And for reward I will give you half of a rice dumpling."

So Momotaro and his vassal went on their way, climbing rough mountains and trudging through shadowy valleys, until just as they reached the outskirts of a thick forest, an immense monkey swung itself downward from a tree and landed in their path.

"Kya! Kya! Kya!" it chattered, with many grimaces. "I demand the rice dumplings in your bag as a penalty for passing through my land."

"Be silent! I am Momotaro on my way to conquer the demons green and red."

The monkey's manner changed at once and he
bent in a humble bow.

"Most honorable Momotaro," he said, "your
name is known to all Monkeyland. I beg you to
permit me to be your humble follower."

"I consent. And for reward I will give you half
of a rice dumpling."

They were about to start on their way when the
dog jumped forward with a fierce growl.

"Go away, you monkey," he snarled. "Go away!"

The monkey sprang to a tree branch and sat
there, chattering and scolding.

"Dog," commanded Momotaro, "march ahead in
silence. Monkey, walk in the rear."

Thus Momotaro went on his way with his two
vassals.

As they were passing a field, a large pheasant flew
from behind a bush. It was a beautiful bird with
rainbow wings and on its head a scarlet cap.

"Chi-ru! Chi-ru!" it shrieked, as it swept through
the air in wide graceful circles. "Give me rice balls,
or I'll peck out your eyes."

Momotaro smiled.

"Be silent. I am Momotaro on my way to conquer the demons green and red."

The bird came fluttering down and sank to the ground in a deep bow.

"Most honorable Momotaro," it chirped, "all Birdland knows your name. I beg you to allow me to accompany you on your journey."

"I consent. And for reward I will give you half of a rice dumpling."

They were about to start, when the growling of the dog before and the chatter of the monkey in the rear frightened the timid bird.

"Silence!" ordered Momotaro in a loud voice. "I am commander, and I give three strict orders. Dog—remember that when warriors quarrel, the battle is lost. Monkey—remember that unity is the key to victory. Pheasant—remember that when enemies work together their purpose cannot fail."

All three, hushed and humbled, bowed before their master. Then Momotaro and his three vassals started peacefully on their way.

The journey was long and hard, but finally they reached a sandy beach where a small boat was rocking on the waves. They looked across the green sea.

The waters tossed and rolled in the sunlight, but not a single island was in sight. The dog, the monkey, and the pheasant were accustomed to the mountain, the forest, and the plain, but none had ever seen the sea before; so they were afraid and began to murmur.

Momotaro turned toward them a scornful face.

"Cowards!" he shouted. "If you fear the sea, why did you ever start for the Demon Island? I do not need you. Go back to your homes!"

He turned from them.

"Honorable Momotaro, we repent!" cried all three as with one voice. "Forgive us and test us. Forevermore we will be brave!"

"I forgive you for the last time," said Momotaro sternly. "From now on—be brave! Success was never won by a coward."

Then Momotaro with his loyal army of three entered the boat and pushed from the shore. The sail filled with wind and the boat cut the waves as an arrow flies through the air. They sailed day after day, sometimes weary and discouraged, but always watching—watching—for the Demon Island. At last, far in the distance they saw a ridge of rocks. Beyond, on top of a high hill, was a wall closed with gates of iron, and a castle with a roof of green and red.

Momotaro stood erect in the bow of the boat.

"Pheasant!" he commanded, "open your wings! Fly to the demons of green and red and tell them that Momotaro from the Land of the Rising Sun is here to fight and conquer them."

"I obey," replied the bird, and spreading his wings he soared higher and higher, until he was above the island, then over the wall, and at last he alighted on the castle roof.

"Listen, ye demons of green and red!" he shrilly called. "Listen! Beyond your gates is Momotaro of the Land of the Rising Sun. He has come to conquer you. If your lives you wish to save, break off your horns and make your humble bow to him. Obey, or you will regret!"

The big demons laughed loud and long.

"Ha-ho-o! Ho-o! Listen to the squawking of the bird! Little one, do you see our great iron clubs? Behold, then fly away in fear!" And they laughed again.

The pheasant was afraid, but it remembered the word of its master; that success never comes to a coward. It bravely ruffled its rainbow feathers and, holding high its red-capped head, it darted downward and gave a sharp peck right between the horns to the biggest demon of them all.

With an astonished shout, the demon raised his iron club, but the bird darted away and lighted on another, and another, striking with quick, sharp pecks that started the demons running here and there, dodging and yelling angrily. In a moment the whole place was a battlefield of roars and shouts, of swinging iron clubs and darting flashes of color. In the meantime, Momotaro, with the dog and the monkey, had left the boat, and running up the hill had rushed through the gate and sprung upon the demons green and red. The whirling iron clubs were strong, but the giants were so big and clumsy that they could not keep pace with the alert, swift-moving foe. So it was not long before, breathless and cowed, they sank to their knees in humble bows to their conquerors.

Then came forward several demons bearing boxes of treasures. They were led by a huge creature who was half green and half red. The monster bowed low, sobbing and with great tears rolling down his cheeks.

"Most brave and honorable Momotaro," he said in a deceitful trembling voice, "we have been wicked demons. We have stolen treasures and killed many people. We have wronged the Land of the Rising Sun, but now that we see how brave are her people, her animals and her birds, we repent and promise hereafter to pay humble homage. We offer these gifts and beg that we be allowed to remain on our island in peace."

"I accept these gifts but only as proper compensation," said Momotaro haughtily. "As you say you wish to become an island of peace, I will take back with me the king of the demons; for well I know there will be no peace if this powerful disturber be left behind."

There was nothing to do but submit, but it was with groans and wailing that the king was bound with a rope and placed in charge of the monkey who, as a guard, carried a big wooden hammer as a weapon. Then a cart was heaped with gifts. These were products of the island—most of them unknown to the Land of the Rising Sun. There were branches of coral, gem-caskets filled with pearls, jade and crystal, and rolls and rolls of brocade, silk and crepe. The dog pulled the cart, the pheasant

carried the banner of Victory, and Momotaro marched proudly, with his war fan spread wide and his fur-covered sword swinging by his side.

Thus did Japan's first hero go forth to conquer and subdue a foreign foe; and thus did he and his brave vassals return with hostage and treasure.

And never more was the Land of the Rising Sun troubled by demons green and red.

Congratulation!   Congratulation!

The Good-Luck Teakettle

FROM

PICTURE TALES FROM THE JAPANESE

By Chiyono Sugimoto

In the olden times there lived a good old priest in a village temple on the edge of a forest. His religion was very strict, but he was allowed to observe the art of "Ceremonial Tea" because it taught self-control. The old priest was devoted to this graceful accomplishment, and during his many years of priesthood had collected, one by one, a very rare and beautiful tea service, every article of which was a treasure of artistic workmanship.

One morning he started out on his priestly duty with his metal gong and hammer in his hand, and a bag for small donations of rice over his shoulder.

"I will have ceremonial tea tonight," he said to a boy-priest. "Have everything ready when I return."

So, toward evening, the boy-priest brought the tea service to the priest's room. While arranging the things, he noticed a slight blemish on the shining surface of a beautiful bronze teakettle. With a piece of soft silk he began to rub it off, watching with pleasure the velvety luster deepening as he rubbed. Presently he thought he heard a soft murmur, which seemed to come from the kettle. He stopped in surprise, but hearing nothing more, he was soon rubbing away harder than ever.

Again he heard the murmuring, and it seemed to keep time to the rub, rub, rub of the polishing cloth. He rubbed slowly, listening. Did he imagine the words?

> "Little priest! Little priest!
> Rub not so hard!
> Rub not so hard!
> The force of thy arm hurts much—
> Hurts much—hurts much!"

The boy rubbed hard for a moment—then stopped and listened. Again came the soft murmur:

"Hurts much! Hurts much!"

And the kettle began to move slowly away from the boy's grasp. A moment more and a furry little head peeped out from one of the polished sides, and a bushy tail from the other. Next, four small legs appeared, and the bronze teakettle had become a tiny badger with an old, old face. The astonished boy called loudly for help.

Several boy-priests came running, and were amazed to see a queer kettle moving by itself across the floor. Then what a chase there was! The little thing ran clumsily, but was very skillful in avoiding the boys as they darted here and there, striking with the bamboo handles of brooms and dusters.

"We have it!" shouted one, as the uncanny little creature wobbled into a corner and came to a stand. Then right before their eyes, the head seemed to slowly melt into the body, and the next moment the badger had disappeared and there stood only a little bronze teakettle.

When the priest returned, the boy-priests gathered about him in great excitement to tell of their strange experience.

"Nonsense!" laughed the priest, thinking the boys had imagined that the kettle moved and had exaggerated in telling the story. Giving no heed to their anxious protests, he put the kettle on the charcoal firebox.

"Look! It is moving again!" whispered one boy-priest to another. And sure enough, in a few moments the kettle was rolling from side to side. Presently out popped a little head, and an aged badger with a plump little body jumped down from the firebox.

"Ya-a, taihen!—Extraordinary!" gasped the priest. And again there was a chase. Priest and pupils ran after the wobbling little thing which skillfully evaded them until, just as the priest was about to grasp it, suddenly it turned into a teakettle.

The next morning a curio dealer happened to come to the temple to ask if there were any treasures to sell or exchange. The puzzled priest thought that it was a good chance to get rid of the troublesome teakettle, so he sold it gladly.

Many times that day the curio dealer congratulated himself upon his good fortune in securing

such a rare and beautiful specimen of art, and he had many pleasant visions of selling it to some rich collector for far more than he had paid for it. When night came he placed the treasure near his bed where it would be safe, and then he fell asleep. About midnight he was awakened by a voice close to his ear.

"Master! Master!" it called softly.

The dealer, half asleep, listened lazily for a moment, then opening his eyes he was amazed to see that his recent purchase was no longer a teakettle, but a funny little animal having a round body of shining bronze with a head on one side and a tail on the other.

"Have I lost my mind?" he cried, springing upright on his bed cushions and grasping his wooden pillow ready to fight if the creature threatened him.

But there was no danger. The odd little thing turned gently toward him and respectfully bowed its head.

"Master," it said, "I am not wholly a teakettle."

The man was half frightened, but looking into the shiny eyes of the little badger, he saw such a gentle expression that his fear changed to curiosity. Pulling his night lantern nearer he pushed the pith wick further out of the oil, and looked carefully at the strange object.

"Well, Teakettle," he finally said, "what is your business?"

The little creature drew a deep sigh of relief.

"Assuredly, I am fortunate," it said, "that a kind fate has dropped me into your hands. When people first saw me, they lost their wits, and drove me away with blows. I did not have a chance to tell them what I am."

The man smiled.

"I always deal fairly with everyone who speaks up frankly," he said. "Tell me your story."

Encouraged by these kind words the kettle began.

"Once I was only a kettle, but I was fashioned by an artist, and no one ever beheld me without a throb of pleasure. And so, during the many, many years of my existence, I have always been handled with gentle and affectionate care. As you know, it is a law of the Great Universe that no emotion is wasted; thus from loving touches my soul was born."

"Hum! Hum!" said the curio dealer. "This is strange indeed! Hum! Hum!"

"For a long time," went on the teakettle, "I was

still a piece of bronze, but a soul was held within. Then heaven poured into my spirit the desire to grow higher, and this holy ambition touched my bronze body with life. So here I am."

"Well! Well!" exclaimed the man, greatly interested. "This is a remarkable tale, but I don't yet know after all, which you are—kettle or badger."

"I can be either."

As he spoke the badger slowly melted into a kettle, returning in a moment to the form of a badger.

"I know nothing of the world," it said, "but now that I have life, I feel the pain of blows and the heat of fire. This makes my future very uncertain. Nevertheless I am happy, for I can take a part in the living world."

"But what can you do, Teakettle—or Badger—whichever you are?"

"I can do many things. I look like a teakettle, but I can walk and run. I can climb a tree or even dance on a slender rope. I can perform any tricks that a trained badger can do, and also I can change myself any moment into either a teakettle or a badger."

The curio dealer pondered deeply for a few moments, the queer little creature watching him with anxious eyes. Finally he reached across for his tobacco box, and thoughtfully pushing aside the ashes of the firebox, he lighted his pipe. After a few slow whiffs an idea seemed to come, for suddenly he laughed aloud.

"I'll offer you a bargain," he cried gleefully. "I've seen these trained badger shows, and if you will do your part, I'll do mine. We'll become famous."

Then he told his plan, to which the badger heartily agreed.

The next morning the dealer sold his curios and bought himself the costume of a cheap theatre manager. Then he engaged a street booth and hired two musicians. The following day when he appeared upon the stage with a queer little round teakettle having a tiny head on one side and a bushy tail on the other, such crowds gathered around the booth that the street carts and men with shoulder poles could scarcely get by.

The tricks the wonderful teakettle played were so many and so strange, that the performances were a success from the beginning. Those who had once seen the show told their friends, and those who could afford it came again and again. The audiences grew larger day by day, and every night the manager found his cashbox heavy with iron coins.

After playing for weeks before great crowds, they left the town and traveled through the country from village to village, until the fame of the queer little dancing kettle spread throughout the land.

Thus many busy months passed by. Both the stage manager and the kettle performer were happy, one with growing riches, the other with a comfortable, active life, and a future of hope.

By and by, when the curio dealer had accumulated more money than he had ever expected to own in his lifetime, he began to think of other things; for he was by nature a thoughtful, kindly man.

"The world is full of strange happenings," he mused one day. "I am made rich and comfortable by a little being lower than myself and yet so cheerful and hopeful that it is a constant lesson to me. I wonder if in the rounds of life, it could be helped on its way."

For many weeks he reflected over this, and finally he had a long and earnest conversation with his little friend.

A few days later, the two started on a journey back to the temple where the little bronze kettle had come to life. The priest had never forgotten the bronze teakettle, and he listened, first with astonishment, and then with grave attention, to the whole story of the badger.

"These riches," the man said in closing, as he spread out a great pile of coin, "have been saved by my friend, the Kettle-Badger and myself. We wish to divide it into equal parts. One half we will present to the temple, with the understanding that the Kettle-Badger is to have the benefit of your holy readings and prayers to help him on his upward way."

The temple accepted the offering, and there the man left his little friend. A small shrine was built in the temple yard to which the priest gave the name of Bun-puku-chagama, which means "Intelligent good-luck teakettle"—and there it stands to-day, just outside the village of Tatebayashi, in the province of Kotsuku. To any inquiring traveler, be he pilgrim or tourist, the simple villagers tell this story; always closing with the words of the Great Buddha, "In thoughtfulness and kindness lie responsibility; for even a stone, if polished with interest and care, will grow more beautiful."

Congratulation!   Congratulation!

Urashima

FROM

PICTURE TALES FROM THE JAPANESE

By Chiyono Sugimoto

In the olden, olden time there lived in the little village of Suminoe a young fisherman by the name of Urashima. One summer evening he was walking homeward from the nearby market town, an empty fish basket slung over his shoulder and a long cloth purse swinging heavily from his girdle. As he crossed a stretch of sand which rounded in a broad curve toward the sea, he came upon a group of boys laughing and shouting noisily over a turtle, which they had caught and were teasing in a most cruel manner. When the little captive tried to crawl in one direction, they would push it with sticks forcing it to move in a circle. When, tired and frightened, it shrunk within its shell, they would place it near the water and wait patiently until it ventured out, then, as it was hurrying toward the water, a dozen heartless kicks would send it far up on the sand. The poor creature was surrounded by taunting foes.

Urashima felt a throb of compassion for its helplessness.

"You boys! Do not torment so small a thing," he called.

The laughing boys gave no heed.

"Let it go!" he called again. "Teasing does not profit you."

"It is ours," one replied. "We caught it ourselves."

"We waded in deep," said another, "and our hardship purchased it. Is it not so, all you?"

"Aye, aye, so it is!" replied the others; and the teasing went on.

Urashima watched a few moments, and pity

weighed his heart as heavily as the iron coins did his belt. Loosening his purse he pulled out one of the heavy strings of coins and waved it clumsily in the air.

"Boys, boys, look up to this!" he called. "I will buy your pleasure. I will give you coin."

The boys stopped, and the eldest of the group, after a hasty glance at the others, pointed to the turtle, now on its back, its legs struggling wildly in the air.

"All right! Let it go!" he said. "There is no bravery in teasing a coward creature."

"That is so! Let it go! Let it go!" the boys laughed and shouted together.

Urashima untied the knot of the straw cord and, slipping off the coins, he gave one to each boy. There was a succession of jerky bows and mutters of, "Thank you, Unknown Uncle!" Then in another moment they had scattered in every direction, their straw sandals sounding, "Ba-ta!—Ba-ta!— Ba-ta!" as they ran.

The fisher youth picked up the wriggling turtle and, placing it gently on his bended arm, he soothed it as he walked toward the water.

"You poor turtle!" he whispered. "Our homely

proverb says, 'The life of the turtle is ten thousand years.' That is a good omen for me, since I pay respect to age in saving you.''

Until this moment the frightened turtle had hidden itself close within its shell, but now, seeming to recognize the voice of a friend in the kind tones, the little creature began slowly to reach out its limbs, then, timidly stretching its snake-like neck, it looked up with shining eyes at the face of the fisherman.

Urashima laughed at its awkward movements on his sleeve, then leaning over he let it slip down gently to the damp sand at the edge of the water. In a moment it was swimming rapidly away.

A few days later, when Urashima was out in his boat fishing, he heard in the far distance a soft voice as deep and mellow as the music of the sea.

"Urashima Sama! Urashima Sama!" it called.

He looked all around. Nothing could he see but the sunny sky and the smooth waves rolling in long shining swells toward the shore.

"Urashima Sama! Urashima Sama!" the same voice called again.

Again he looked, but saw only sky and smooth rolls of moving water in the sunshine. Puzzled, he

waited. Presently, in the distance a dark spot appeared. It came nearer and he saw that it was a turtle swimming rapidly toward him. As it approached the boat, it lifted its brown head.

"Urashima Sama," it said, "I am the turtle whose life you saved. I have come to thank you!"

Unconsciously the youth bowed, for there was a dignity in the gentle voice of the homely creature, which caused him to give it respect.

"Also I have brought a message from the Water World," the turtle continued. "Have your ears ever heard of the Dragon Palace?"

"Oh yes," the fisherman replied. "From my youth I have heard the tales of our wise old people about the wonders of the unknown palace."

"Would you like to make a visit there?" the turtle asked. "Our Princess, Oto Hime, the beautiful mistress of the Dragon Palace,"—and the wrinkled neck and brown head of the turtle bowed to the surface of the water in honor of the name so respectfully spoken—"will graciously be pleased to entertain you in return for your kindness to one of her subjects—my humble self."

Urashima was incredulous, and a little fearful,

but he was filled with curiosity.

"How can I go to the Dragon Palace?" he asked.

"I will carry you," replied the turtle. "Pray mount upon my back."

"But you are small. I have held you on my bended arm."

"Pray mount!" repeated the turtle.

Urashima hesitatingly stepped from his boat upon the shining shell, and strangely, as he ventured his weight, the turtle slowly grew larger, until, as he seated himself, he found that he was on a platform of shell almost as large as his fishing boat. Then he was told to close his eyes and sit quietly.

With a smooth, gliding motion they started, increasing the speed each moment until they were moving as swiftly as one flies in a dream. Faster and faster they went, the strange steed sliding over the waves, with the fisherboy sitting erect, his eyes closed and his hands unconsciously clutching his fish rod and his basket. The hot breeze which at first fanned his cheek, changed to a cool, moist touch, and all was silence except the rush of water-sound in his ears. It seemed they had traveled for hours, yet they went on—on—steadily, swiftly—

through the coolness, darkness, and silence. At last they moved more slowly.

"Urashima Sama, behold!" sounded the mellow voice.

The fisherman opened his eyes upon a sight so beautiful that he thought he had reached the heavenly country. In the midst of a world of soft misty light, he could see, in the clear distance, a palace whose graceful, sloping roofs were of rainbow hues and of strange beautiful curves. The crystal walls glittered softly in the cool, blue light, and leading up to the arched gateway was a long avenue of coral trees, the delicate pink branches blossoming with gems of a thousand colors.

The astonished youth gazed and gazed.

"It is the Dragon Palace," sounded the mellow voice. "Listen to your welcome in the music of the sea."

A strange melody throbbed through the waves, clear and beautiful, but weird beyond words. It rose and fell in long swells of sound, beneath which thrilled a song of unknown words.

Slowly they approached the palace, floating silently through the avenue of coral trees, beneath the glittering branches, up to the crystal gateway. A group of maidens, robed in pink and silver-green, with jeweled pins in their glossy hair, met the be- wildered fisher-lad and led him to the Princess, who was seated on a throne of mother-of-pearl. Her robe was of pale green. Pearls and emeralds glistened in her hair, and in their midst, just above her brow, quivered a dragon-shaped spark of living light. It was her soul, unconcealed, as pure as crystal, but held in thrall by a woman's nature—the curse of snake-like shape. Such was the beautiful Dragon Princess, the immortal goddess of purity and love.

Urashima's eyes had never looked upon such beauty; and so gentle and modest was she, and with such dignity did she conduct him to the apartment prepared for him, that in the new wonderful sur- roundings he forgot his parents, his home, and all the world except the Dragon Palace.

For three days he lived in the beautiful World of Water, and the time passed like an hour of happy dreams. Alas! he did not know that the Dragon Palace was also Fuyajo, the Castle of No-Night, and that there a hundred years are as a day.

But at last his sleeping memory awakened, and

remorsefully he thought upon his neglected parents. In haste he went to Oto Hime and told her of his wish to return to his home. The Princess asked him if he were unhappy.

"Oto Hime Sama," he answered, "my soul longs to remain in this beautiful World of the Sea, but my floating boat and half-drawn nets were left behind, and I fear my parents' hearts are torn with anxiety. It is my duty to return and ease their pain."

"Urashima," the Princess slowly replied, "my heart is sad that you must go, but filial duty is the first of all the duties of the world. To the land of your honorable parents you must return."

Then she brought as a farewell gift, a box having a deep overreaching cover. She lifted it reverently to her brow, then handed it to Urashima.

"I have one plea," she said. "I beg you will keep this box until we meet again; but be heedful never to open it, or misfortune will come. Remember."

Then she sent for the turtle, and gave commands to all the palace to prepare for Urashima's departure.

When all was ready, the fisher-lad mounted his steed of shining shell, and placing the mystery box

carefully beneath his arm, he slung his wicker
basket across his shoulder and took his fish rod in
his hand. He bowed deeply in farewell, but before
closing his eyes for the water journey he looked
back once more upon the Dragon Palace.

The beautiful Princess stood in the crystal gateway at the end of the avenue of coral trees with
their glittering jewel blossoms. Her maidens were
kneeling on either side, their glossy heads bowed
to the floor, and the weird music of the sea was
pulsing in mournful waves of farewell. Again the
youth bowed, then closed his eyes and floated
swiftly away. The Princess watched him, the dragon
of light on her brow quivering and paling until
it shone dim and misty amidst the glittering gems,
for the soul of Oto Hime was sad. Well she knew
that the fate of an immortal is ever a hopeless
struggle against loneliness, and that Urashima the
fisher-lad had disappeared from the Water World
forever.

The turtle carried the youth back to the same
sandy shore where they had met long before, and
left him there, gazing wonderingly about him. The
outward curve of the beach had been wave-worn

into a straight line, and the familiar little village of fisher huts just beyond had changed in some mystic manner into a thriving little town of odd-shaped wooden houses. He stood looking about him, dazed with wonder, then slowly approached the town. In his own village everyone was known to everyone else, but as he walked through these streets he saw only strange things and met only unknown people, all wearing peculiar clothing and all staring with wonder at his simple fishing garments.

Puzzled, he turned his steps in the direction of his old home, but he found not one familiar spot. At last, confused and discouraged, he stopped before a door.

"Where am I?" he asked. "Who are these people? How happened this strange change?"

A young woman came slowly forward, looking half-frightened, and hesitatingly gave him the name of his own village. Then she kindly offered him a piece of dried fish and a salted rice-ball, for the poor fisherman looked pale and weak. For a while he sat bowed and silent, then he told the woman he was Urashima and that he had left his home only three days before, and now he had come back to find everything changed.

The woman listened, looking pityingly at him.

"No, my poor man, that cannot be true," she said kindly. "You say you left this village only three days ago? Why, I was born here. I know all who live in the village, and I have never heard of any of the names you mention. You do not look like us. You seem a stranger who has walked out from a picture painted by an ancient artist. You belong elsewhere."

Urashima sighed, and walked hopelessly on. Everywhere he met with hospitality, but it was given with the pity shown to one with a lost mind. Finally the poor lad, weary, puzzled, heart-sad, wandered down to the shore and stood looking upon the only familiar thing in the whole world— the blue waters of the ocean. As he watched the waves tossing bright in the sunlight, they reminded him of the jeweled columns of the Dragon Palace. Then there came to his memory vague, half-lost recollections of a tale heard in his youth, that the palace of the sea was called, "Fuyajo, the Castle of No-Night," because there hundreds of years are as one day.

"These tales must be true," he thought, his heart

clutched with a sudden cold fear, "for here am I—alone! My people, the old customs, all the world of my life, seem to have been buried in past and forgotten ages. What is left for me?"

He threw himself on the sand in despair, and then he noticed the forgotten box beneath his arm —the gift of the Dragon Princess. A wave of joy struck his soul. He forgot all the earnest warnings of Oto Hime. He remembered only the words, "Keep this until we meet again," and joyously placing the box upon the ground, he hastened to untie the silken cord. As he was about to lift the cover, he hesitated, for a strange misgiving weighted his hand.

He cast a glance back at the strange village, and gave one thought to his kind parents whom he had so thoughtlessly forsaken. He looked forward at the blue waves tossing above the beautiful hidden palace, and his heart was filled with longing for the happiness that was gone. Then, slowly and with a deep breath of fear and hope, he lifted the lid.

Softly into the air floated a purple mist. Slowly it arose and folded like a cloud about the youth, wrapping him for an instant in its tinted depths. Then it faded into nothingness, leaving on the sands the lifeless body of an old, faded, wrinkled man, his back bent and his brow white with the snows of age.

Sorrowful!   Sorrowful!

T H E   E N D

3490